MERGERS & ACQUISITIONS

JODI PAYNE

Mergers & Acquisitions
Copyright © 2021 by Jodi Payne

Edited by Flat Earth Editing
https://www.flatearthediting.com/

Cover illustration by Designs by Morningstar
https://morningstarashley.com/
Cover content is for illustrative purposes only and any person depicted on the cover is a model.

ISBN: 978-1-951011-16-1

Electronic edition published by Tygerseye Publishing, LLC, April, 2021
Printed in the USA

1

―――――

Jason stood at the bottom of the stairwell at the 49th Street subway station, psyching himself up for a four-block slog in the pouring rain. Not north and south blocks, of course, but four long-ass avenue blocks. What the hell was going on? It hadn't been raining this hard when he left Brooklyn.

Seriously? This was so gonna suck.

Finally accepting that the rain wasn't going let up anytime soon, he pulled his hood tighter around his face, shrugged his backpack onto both shoulders, and took off at a jog. The deeper he went into Hell's Kitchen, though, the more the wind blew the rain into his face until he found himself trudging along and leaning into it, forehead low, hands stuffed into his pockets for warmth.

He didn't have the cash for the cab ride across the bridge and into the city, but maybe he could find someone who would be into sharing a ride back to Brooklyn once he had some tip money in his pocket.

Assuming he made some money tonight. This crappy

weather might keep people away. Maybe not the tourists, but the locals would probably say to hell with it, stay home and watch porn instead. That was totally what he would do if he wasn't working.

He crossed against the light at Ninth, sprinting the last few feet to get out of the way of a big black SUV with Jersey plates that was honking at him. The asshole was probably headed for the Lincoln Tunnel.

"Screw you, Jersey!" he shouted and flipped the driver off. Wasn't likely they'd see it, but whatever. It made him feel better.

"Jason!"

That had to be Danny. Who else would be running in platform boots and a bright-yellow rain slicker? "Danny! You're ruining those heels in this weather."

"What, these? These are my rain boots, baby." Danny laughed and took his arm.

Jason pulled Danny under the awning of a dry cleaner and smiled. "It's Dallas, by the way."

"Dallas? Are you going away?" Danny looked confused.

"No, my stage name. It's Dallas."

"Really?"

"Or maybe Austin? No, I think it was Dallas." Texan, in any case.

"You're gonna be a cowboy?"

He nodded. "That's what Aaron said he wanted when he hired me."

Danny leaned close, shivering a little even as he giggled. "Well, you've got the guns for it, sweetheart, that's for sure."

"Ha ha." He did, though. The guns, the quads, the abs... he was proud of his body. His rent might be late, but he was always paid up at the gym.

"Let's hear your accent."

Jason laughed. "Okay. Can ah git you a draink, sugar?"

Danny wrinkled his nose. "Oh, baby. That's...wow."

Bad. He knew. "Shut up." They both started laughing. What was he gonna do? The owner wanted a cowboy, and he wanted a job. He'd get better.

"Thanks for getting me the interview." Maybe it wasn't a classy job, but man, did he need the money. Plus, whatever gene it was that kept normal people from being completely shameless? He just wasn't born with it. This could actually turn out to be the perfect job for him.

"I hope it works out for you, baby. I think you're going to do great. Lord knows you can dance."

"Let's hope. We better get moving before we're late."

"Ugh." Danny sighed dramatically. "This fucking weather is murder on my hair." Danny's long, dark hair, which he usually tamed and styled with product, had that beautiful, naturally wavy thing going on. But yeah, the humidity was hell on Jason's short, dirty-blond curls, so he could only imagine the time it took Danny to compensate.

The two of them ran the last half block together arm in arm. They ran right past the main club entrance and stopped by a completely unmarked metal door with no handle on the outside.

Jason squinted up at the marquee through the raindrops. On top of it were the words "The Wiggle Room" in neon pink and green, surrounded by blue chasing lights. He shook his head at himself. Yep. This was for real. He was an entertainer now.

Danny banged on the door with the side of his fist, protecting his bright-yellow nail polish, and one of the biggest men Jason had ever seen opened the door for them.

A barrel chest and tree-trunk arms filled the doorway, completely blocking the view of whatever was inside.

"Come on in, ladies." The guy stepped out of their way.

Jason winked. "That's 'cowboy,' actually."

"Oh, yeah? Yeehaw, then." The security guy didn't even crack a smile.

"Oh, Jackson." Danny gave the man a poke in the chest and looked at Jason. "He's a big softie, baby, don't let him fool you."

"Yippee ki-yay." Jason smiled at Jackson and tipped an imaginary hat. Still not one hint of a smile. *Wow*.

Jackson blinked at him slowly. He'd have bet the man was stoned. "Bruce Willis."

"What?"

"That's not cowboy, that's Bruce Willis."

"Oh. Right." *Shit, I'm too Brooklyn to be a fucking cowboy.* "Thanks."

Danny took his arm. "Come on, baby, let's get you settled."

"Later, cowboy. Welcome to the club."

"Thank you, Jackson." Jason laughed and followed Danny down a narrow hall. Just beyond the entryway was the dressing room he'd seen during his interview. It had rows of lighted mirrors along one wall and several garment racks along another, and men were in various stages of undress as they got ready for work.

"There you are." Aaron's deep voice vibrated in his ears as the club owner crossed the room to him. "Are you ready?"

Jason nodded. "Born ready."

"Yeah?" Aaron seemed happy with that answer. "Guess we'll see, won't we? Come on."

Danny gave Jason a kiss on the cheek. "See you out there, doll."

———

AN HOUR LATER, Jason—*now Dallas*—headed out onto the floor, wearing a pair of frayed cutoff jeans that barely covered his muscled ass cheeks, a belt with a big fake-silver buckle and cheap cowboy boots that squashed the hell out of his toes. Aaron topped that off with a red plaid sleeveless shirt that Jason buttoned closed over his chest but left open closer to his beltline. Had to leave something to the imagination, right? On his head sat a dollar-store, straw cowboy hat, and for later when he got some stage time, he also had a lasso and a pair of gloves back in the dressing room. Not that he had the faintest idea how to use a fucking lasso. Maybe he'd learn.

Ha. Please. You're too Brooklyn to lasso, too.

Yeah, that wasn't going to happen. There wasn't enough elbow room anywhere in the city for him to learn to twirl that thing, anyway.

He probably should have felt like a clown, but for some reason he fucking *loved* it. He couldn't wait until he had enough money to buy some boots that fit. Maybe he'd been a cowboy in a past life. He totally believed in all of that Buddhist reincarnation stuff. Or was it Hindu reincarnation stuff? Whatever it was, he was totally into it.

His job while on the floor was to schmooze, offer drinks, and basically work the room, so guys would be more interested in him when he was on stage. But Aaron told him that lap dances were the way to make real money. They weren't required, but Aaron had let him watch a few through a one-way security mirror when he came in for his interview in case he decided he was interested.

Well, fuck yeah, he was interested in anything that would make him some "real money."

He'd spent a ridiculous amount of time on YouTube and Tumblr trying to learn how to give a good one, and he'd practiced with one of his kitchen chairs. He'd even practiced on a couple of his roommates, who'd laughed their asses off at him but enjoyed his efforts all the same.

Especially Ricky. Shit, that boy was a slut for anyone. Jason smiled at the thought. He liked Ricky. They were a lot alike that way.

Jason hadn't been on the floor for five minutes when he felt guys checking him out. He smiled and glanced back, but most of them looked away if he tried to catch their eye. Some of them were probably embarrassed to be caught ogling, but some of them, he was pretty sure, knew he was trolling for lap dances, and they weren't into paying him for one.

He got that. Ten bucks cover just to get in the door, eight or nine bucks a drink—it wasn't a cheap neighborhood bar, that was for sure. Add on more for a private dance plus a tip, and it was practically an investment.

God knew he couldn't afford to get in the door himself.

"Hey. Cowboy!"

There was a whistle and Jason looked around, spotting three men off to his left gathered around a cocktail table. One of them was waving him down.

Show time.

Jason gave them a big, flirty smile, put a hand on his chest, and mouthed, *Me?* He totally had this.

One of them stuck two fingers in his mouth and whistled at him again. Jason squared his shoulders, puffed his chest, and made his way over, slowly enough that they could get a good look at him. "Howdy, boys."

He'd watched a ton of westerns to prepare for this gig, and yesterday he'd listened to Kenny Chesney's entire fucking catalog. There wasn't any way his Brooklyn-born ass would pass for a real cowboy, but he could fake it for city boys and tourists.

"Love your hat."

"Thank you, sir." Jason tipped it at the tall blond closest to him. "I'm Dallas. Y'all havin' a good time?"

They all nodded at him, and when he asked what they were drinking, they let him order them another round. That was a damn good way to start.

"So where y'all from?"

"New Jersey," the blond said. "But these guys are from Michigan. They're getting married."

Oh, that was money right there.

"What? Well, doesn't that just dill my pickle. Congrat-u-lations!"

They all laughed, making Jason feel braver.

"Thank you." One of the grooms gave him a shy smile, and Jason ran with it.

"Aw, aren't you sweet? What's your name, honey?"

"Adam."

Jason smiled. "Pleased, Adam." He gave a nod, then looked at the other groom, glad they were from Michigan and not Texas. They'd laugh him right out of the bar.

"And you, sugar? What do they call you?"

"I'm Philip." Philip seemed a little less shy and a little more interested.

"Philip and Adam. And when are you boys tying it up?"

The tall blond from New Jersey spoke up. "Tomorrow at city hall."

"Well, honey...what's your name?"

"Devon."

"Well, Devon, I'm thinking a truly good friend would

buy these lovebirds a little down-home bachelor party entertainment. Am I right?"

The blond laughed. "That's exactly why we called you over here, cowboy."

Jason hooted. "Well, all righty, then. Who's first, boys? Or should we make it a double?"

2

_____

No one had been interested in sharing a cab home that first night, but Jason had sprung for one anyway even though the rain had stopped. He'd gone home high on adrenaline and with more cash in his pocket than he'd ever seen in one place in his whole life.

He'd spread it out on his bed and counted it three times. He'd totally felt like Daddy Warbucks.

"So, *Dallas*." Danny played with his stage name and glanced over at him from the mirror next to his. "It's been two whole weeks now. Isn't this about the time you usually quit a new job?"

Jason snorted. "Usually." He wasn't so good with holding down jobs he didn't like. But he'd try anything, so he was rarely out of work.

"And you're still here so...you like it?"

He did like it. "I love it. Love. It." He was good at it. It seemed to just come naturally. And it was fun.

Jason had been spending nearly all his free time sleeping or studying cowboys. He found an iHeartRadio country station. He watched movies. He went online and studied cowboy lingo. He was obsessed. It was ridiculous, he knew—no one at the club actually expected him to be anything like a *real* cowboy, but the more he learned about them, the more he wished he'd been born one.

He'd completely romanticized the idea in his mind. Somehow it seemed way better to be a broke cowboy in a country song, driving a beat-up pickup on a red dirt road than to be...well, just another hardworking straphanger from Brooklyn.

His cowboy accent still sucked, though, and he'd decided he was better off just looking like a cowboy, not trying to sound like one.

"Yeah? It's not bad, right? Kind of hell too, though."

Jason shrugged. "It's hard work for sure, but it's *fun*."

He worked his freakin' ass off, in fact, and by the time his shift was over his feet were always killing him, his back sometimes hurt, and he usually smelled worse than he did after his longest day at the gym. But he'd made his rent money and then some in just a few nights, and cash was addictive.

At first, he'd saved every penny he could because the blisters from his cheap pair of boots were unreal. They wept and bled, and his feet looked like hamburger. They hurt like hell all the time, too. And all the gauze and bandages he needed to cover the blisters didn't make them fit any better.

But man, he was one happy camper. He could do this. He totally could.

Danny smiled at him. "I thought you might be good at this gig."

"I hope so. Oh! Did I show you my new boots?" He was so excited. He couldn't wait to show them off tonight.

"No. Did you go shopping?"

"Wait. Look." Jason slid off his chair and went to his locker to get his new prize possessions. "The sales guy said they were made in El Paso and they're goat leather. Aren't they amazing?"

"Oh, my God, Jase. Those are gorgeous." Danny looked at him. "Expensive, huh?"

He blushed, feeling a little embarrassed. "Yeah. I dropped nearly an entire month's rent on them. But they waterproofed them for me because you know, people spill drinks and stuff. I know it seems ridiculous, but they are so comfortable. I could dance all night."

He adored them.

"Not so ridiculous. I have some of my dance shoes custom fitted too. You can't be sexy and look like you're having fun if your feet are covered in blisters."

"Right?" Oh, Jason was glad to hear Danny say that. He felt way better about the expense now. "They'll last forever, too."

The salespeople taught him how to break them in, and he carefully followed their instructions. His boots were the biggest investment in anything he'd ever made. He ended up wearing them almost nonstop—on all of his errands, everywhere. They were too cool not to show off some, and he wanted them comfortable. This would be the first night he wore them at work.

He bought a couple of other fun things for his costume while he was downtown, too. A metal belt buckle that said "Cowboy Up" above a longhorn skull with big, wide horns, and a new straw hat that fit his head and looked great.

"I wanted some Wranglers, but I couldn't bring myself to buy them just to cut them into shorts."

Danny laughed. "You're really throwing yourself into this. No wonder Aaron likes you so much. Keep checking the thrift places. You might find some that are shorts already."

Oh, that was a great idea. If...*wait*. "Did you say Aaron likes me?" That was good to know.

Danny nodded. "Just keep doing what you're doing."

"You know, I never asked you how long you've worked here."

"A year." Danny shrugged. "It's good money; it's kind of hard to give that up."

"Yeah, I hear that."

He and Danny chatted while they dressed for their shift. He was always going to be a cowboy, at least until Aaron said he wasn't, but Danny was harder to pin down. Danny was... pretty. Heels and feather boas, hot pants and false eyelashes. Lots of color. Flirty. Whatever it was, it worked. Danny looked great and people loved him.

They stepped out on the floor together, immediately turning heads. "This is where we part ways, honey. You have a good night. Be so good you're bad."

"Later." Jason laughed and walked farther into the room. He'd learned a lot in the last couple of weeks—who to look out for, who to spend some time with, and who to just wave at and move on. It wasn't that hard; he was good at reading people.

Tonight, Jason was looking to make some bucks. He had rent coming up again, but it was more than that. He'd decided to see if he could save some money for...something. A rainy day, a trip, or something new for his bedroom. Or just to put something in the bank. To finally have that feeling that he was okay. That if something happened, he wouldn't have to worry about his next paycheck for a while. A little nest egg so he could breathe.

It was good to have a goal.

He adjusted his hat and his smile and went looking for some tips.

3

"Tough break on the Avenstone deal, Whitaker."

"Yeah, thanks." Teague nodded. Tough break? It was more than a tough break; it was a fucking disaster. Likely a career-ending fucking disaster, at least with this firm. He was sure Carson realized that, but he supposed the guy was trying to be supportive.

"You want to get a drink?"

Yes. He definitely wanted a drink, but not with Carson. Not with anyone.

"Thanks, I'm good. I'm pretty wiped out."

"Sure, man. I hear you." Carson lingered in his office doorway for another second as if he wanted to say something else, but instead he rapped his knuckles on Teague's doorjamb and said good night.

Thank God.

Teague packed up his briefcase and set it on his desk. He looked at it for a minute and decided to just leave it there, tucking his wallet and his phone into his pockets. What did he need the paper work for tonight? He didn't have a fireplace to burn it in.

Okay, he was getting sour now. It was time for that drink.

He left his office and managed to resist the urge to turn back and look it over in case he didn't get to see it again. That was probably a tad melodramatic. Probably.

It was a warm night and still pretty light out for seven thirty, with summer almost over and fall not quite taking hold yet. He walked for a while, just breathing and trying to get his head around what had happened. He'd been over it ten times already at least, but he went through it all again because no matter how he did the math for himself, no matter what he figured into the equation, it just didn't add up for him.

He hadn't blown the deal. He was confident of that. He was a good attorney—better than good—and had been working almost exclusively on this acquisition for Avenstone for months. He'd been clear on his client's priorities, and he'd negotiated everything to their satisfaction. He'd worked around the goddamn clock for the last week to get all of the agreements hammered out and drafted, and then one damn day before closing the sellers had tried to renegotiate one of the key terms. Teague consulted his client, they stood their ground, and the deal just collapsed out from under him.

Dissolved. Evaporated. It just *died*.

The fact was, this kind of shit happened all the time in his business. You negotiated, and you either reached a deal or you didn't. Carson was right; it was a tough break. But Teague felt like this one was more than he could reasonably handle. Avenstone was frustrated, and they'd gone right over Teague to the head of the practice. Teague was convinced he'd lost the client.

Regardless, he could kiss that partner track good-bye.

Maybe he ought to have let Carson buy him that drink

after all. Maybe he could have asked for some advice. Or at least the number of Carson's headhunter. But Teague wasn't up for soothing Carson's survivor guilt tonight. Carson had a pretty solid book of business and had been kicking corporate M&A ass. He was practically closing shit in his sleep.

Goddamn it. He needed that drink. Now.

He'd been walking east into Hell's Kitchen from his office in Times Square, toward those places he frequented when he was in a certain mood and wanted to drink alone. There were plenty of bars that were better suited for socializing when he wanted to. Places with a nice bar, a neighborhood feel, a friendly bartender. Places where he could hang out and meet people. Meet men. Have a good time.

Most of those places didn't have a cover, and the drinks were reasonable—well, reasonable for New York. But he didn't give a shit about the money, and friendly wasn't what he was looking for tonight. Tonight he wanted to look, to watch, to be entertained. Distracted. He wanted out of his head, to fantasize. He didn't want to know anyone, and he wanted to be able to pay some hot dancer good money just to pour him into a cab and send him home alone once he got drunk enough that he couldn't stand up.

He walked past one club and then another, settling on one he'd only been to a couple of times. The Wiggle Room had a reputation for walking the razor's edge. The place also had a reputation for being hard to get into, so he straightened his jacket but loosened his tie and opened a button at his throat. He ran his fingers through his dark hair as he stood in the entrance line, working on that rakish-but-loaded vibe, wanting to look like he was ready to spend his money.

"You're alone?" The bouncer looked him over, head to toe.

"Yes."

"ID?"

"Rough day, looking to have a drink, and blow off some steam." Teague pressed a fifty into the guy's palm along with his license, and the guy gave him his ID right back and stamped his hand.

"Came to the right place."

"I'm sure of it." Teague made his way inside. The music was loud, the dance floor busy, and the bar was lit up and crowded. He made his way over to see if he could find a spot to settle, and he was finally able to shoulder in right as a couple moved away. He slid onto a barstool that was still warmed by the ass that had just left it.

He pulled out his credit card and set it on the bar in front of him, and a bartender was over in an instant. One of four behind the bar tonight.

"Whiskey sour."

The bartender was a fine specimen of man. Easily six feet plus with broad shoulders. His muscle top was tight, and his shorts were tighter. "Tab?"

Teague nodded.

"Stockbroker, honey?"

"I beg your pardon?" Teague looked over at the young man in the cowboy hat who'd appeared at his side, noticing right off how stacked the guy was. Short, but well-built, a good couple of inches shorter than Teague. A sleeveless shirt showed off major biceps, and the guy's thighs seemed ready to pop right out of his cutoffs.

"Wall Street?" The cowboy asked and leaned an elbow on the bar.

"God, no."

"How about...investment banker?"

"Nope."

"Market analyst?"

He snorted. "How long are you going to keep this up?"

"Until you tell me." The cowboy's smile was flirtatious and coy.

Teague raised an eyebrow. "Attorney." A soon-to-be unemployed one.

"Well, I'll be. I could've kept right on guessing. I'd've got it eventually, but you don't look like a man with a whole lot of patience right now."

The cowboy had that right. "Tie gave me away, huh?"

"Nah, the perfect hair." The guy reached for Teague's already loose tie and slowly untied the knot entirely, rolled the silk fabric around one hand, and stuffed it into Teague's jacket pocket. "There. Now, doesn't that feel better?"

Teague knew the game here; this pretty dancer with the brilliant smile wanted him to shell out big bucks for a private lap dance. Everybody had to make a living, right? "It does."

Teague's drink arrived, and the cowboy nodded approvingly. "What's your name, Wall Street?"

"I'm an attorney. I actually work in Midtown, not in the financial district." Why the hell did that even matter? He wasn't interested in small talk.

The cowboy shrugged. "All the same to me, honey. I'm Dallas."

Dallas. Sure. If the man was born below the Mason-Dixon line, it wasn't any farther south than Baltimore. He was more like good old down-home Jersey City. "Teague."

"What kind of name is Teague?"

"It's Irish." His name actually meant "handsome," which

he'd tried to use a few times as a pickup line, but it had never worked.

"May I?" Dallas lifted the cherry from his glass and dangled it between his fingers.

"Sure."

The cowboy smiled at him and caught the cherry with his teeth and tugged off its stem. "Ooh. Leon's givin' you the good stuff right off." Dallas licked his mischievous fingers.

Of course he was. Teague was a man with cash to burn who probably looked like he knew a good whiskey. Leon wanted to make a buck too, right? A couple of drinks in, Leon would switch to the cheap shit, figuring Teague would be just drunk enough not to notice.

Well, the joke was on Leon. Teague didn't actually know a thing about whiskey, except that it burned just right going down and was going to help him forget his day. Leon could have given him the cheap shit right off the bat, and he'd have neither noticed nor cared. He picked up his drink, took a long gulp, and loosened another button on his shirt.

"That's it, honey, relax. Let your long day go."

Teague looked at Dallas and gave him a wink. "Not drunk enough yet, Jersey cowboy. Try me again in an hour."

"That's Dallas to you, partner. *Dallas*. And I'm living in Brooklyn nowadays." Dallas winked at him. "Talk doesn't cost a thing, you know."

"I don't have much to say."

"Well. Then you drink, and I'll talk." The dancer braced a foot on his stool and hopped right up, planting his ass on the bar and bringing everything from those narrow hips down into view.

Teague wanted to touch the muscled thighs, but he knew better. You didn't do that unless you were ready to get thrown out. He could look, though, and he did, then lifted his glass in salute and took another sip.

"So. A hot guy in a nice suit comes in on a weeknight, wanting whiskey. There's no good story behind that."

"Yeah, well." He shrugged. That was the truth.

Dallas planted one snub-toed fancy boot on Teague's barstool, right between his legs. Jersey cowboy had some sweet boots. He didn't realize you could make that kind of cash in a place like this.

"I guess you're fixin' to forget your day."

"Big-time."

He'd kind of like to forget his whole week. Maybe the whole damn month. What the hell was he going to do tomorrow? Should he show up at the office? And do what? Sit at his desk and stare at the walls until someone came in and gently—or not so gently—let him go? He couldn't imagine any other scenario. It was possible, he supposed, that they'd throw some busywork at him just to be kind, maybe see if he'd try to bring in anyone else, but that would waste their time, and his, too. He wouldn't take that offer.

He could find another job, but how quickly? Should he even put this one on his résumé? What kind of reference would he get from his current firm?

Fuck, he'd come here for a distraction. "Can we talk about something else?"

"Sure, honey. How's your—"

"Gentlemen!"

"Oh, boy." Dallas winked at him, and Teague raised an eyebrow.

"Oh, boy?"

"Straight outta Texas, everyone give it up for the beautiful boy from the Lone Star State, The Wiggle Room's own yellow rose. It's *Dallas*!"

"Kiss me."

"What?" Had he heard that right?

A spotlight hit the bar as the music started, making Teague squint, and the next thing he knew, Dallas had a hand behind his head and was kissing him. Teague was so startled, he just kissed the cowboy right back. A shiver shot up his spine and as Dallas pulled away, Teague got a look into the cowboy's moss-green eyes.

Dallas laughed and winked, delighted, and stood right up on the bar as the first verse kicked in.

No longer in the spotlight, Teague ran his fingers over his lips slowly, feeling himself smile. What the hell was that? He shook it off and scooped up his drink again, swallowing most of it in one more gulp as the country song grew louder. It wasn't anything he recognized, but it had a great beat, a steel guitar, and a woman was singing about leaving her man and his cheating ways.

Teague approved.

"Another?" Teague nodded at Leon, watching Dallas shake his hips like Shakira as he made his way to the far end of the bar. Teague approved of that, too.

Once Dallas hit the end of the bar, he was helped down by a burly bouncer, and Teague suddenly caught on.

He'd been targeted. He'd been part of that cowboy's show since hello.

Teague grinned and shook his head at himself. Sometimes he could be so gullible. He started to look around to see who might try to make him their next victim, but his eyes kept going back to Dallas, making his way, escorted by a couple of bouncers, to the oval stage. The stage floor was lit from underneath, colors fading from one to the next as the lights shifted to the beat of the music. But the bright spotlight stuck to the dancer like glue. Dallas's checkered shirt fell to the stage floor first, and Teague's breath caught for a second in his chest. The dancer removed a heavy belt, starting with a big belt buckle, and opened the top button of barely-there cutoffs to reveal a black elastic waistband.

Teague exhaled, eyes glued to the dancer as Dallas turned his back to the crowd. Someone tossed a bill up on the stage, and Dallas bent over and picked it up between his legs, sticking his muscular ass right in the guy's face. The guy reached up and slapped one of Dallas's denim-covered cheeks, and Teague snorted as the bouncers swooped in and literally carried the idiot to the door.

"No touching" was more than just good etiquette. It was a rule in most clubs. Look all you like, hoot, holler and whistle, throw money and beg for more, but don't ever touch. This wasn't a dive strip-club after all, and the dancers knew their business. This was a classy place. It was likely that no one here got naked. Not even in private.

Dallas turned around and waved good-bye to the guy with the crisp, green bill before shrugging, grinning, and making a show of putting the money into his pocket. Several more bills joined the first, littering the stage floor, and Dallas blew kisses; then he turned around again and rocked with the music, lowering his cutoffs inch by inch over his round ass, over his thick thighs, until finally they were able to fall to the floor on their own.

Teague shook his head as a handful of bills joined the ones already littering the stage. It was a wonder Dallas could just leave them there, but Teague figured no one was going to touch them. Especially after watching someone get bounced.

Underneath his cutoffs, Dallas had on a black thong, and Teague couldn't help but admire the man's pumped-up glutes. Jesus Christ, that dancer was in good fucking shape. It actually took effort for Teague not to drool. Watching the guy turn around didn't help matters either. Dallas was well-endowed, his prick easily filling and stretching the black material.

The music came to an end, and Dallas turned around again and slapped himself on the ass.

Teague grinned and joined in the applause, whistling through his fingers and clapping his hands as Dallas grinned and bowed and scooped up his tips. "Yeehaw! Dallas!"

He turned on his stool as another dancer took the stage. He'd watch again in a little while, but right now there was wrestling on TV behind the bar and he had whiskey to drink. He lifted his glass and took a long sip.

Someone near him smelled great. Versace Eros and... something. Teague looked over and a man in a tight white T-shirt and blue jeans smiled at him.

Well, well.

Teague returned the smile and lifted his glass just in time for some other guy to whisk his potential company away to the dance floor.

What?

Damn.

He finished his second drink and was on this third when Dallas the dancing cowboy showed up at his elbow.

"Drunk enough yet, sugar?" Well, what d'you know? Dallas's fake drawl sounded much more convincing to Teague with a couple of drinks in him.

Teague laughed. "You have clothes on. How disappointing."

Dallas nodded, grinning. "Sounds like that's a yes."

"You have thighs like boulders, cowboy."

"Thank you, kindly. He may be small, yet he is mighty."

Teague laughed. " 'Though she be but little, she is fierce.' "

"She who?"

He was pretty sure Dallas was playing with him, but he was also pretty drunk. "Hermia, Helena? One of those H people."

"Horny?" Dallas winked.

"Yes." Teague shook his head. "Uh. I mean no. That's not in Shakespeare. I mean, yes there's a lot of *that* in Shakespeare, horny people, I mean, but not the name 'Horny.' Not precisely."

The dancer stared at him, grinning. "Wow."

Teague pushed his glass a few inches away. "Uh, yeah. Maybe I'm cut off."

"Maybe you need a little cowboy-sized VIP treatment, Wall Street."

"Not going to argue with you, Dallas. Gonna hit the men's room first, though." He needed a minute to sober up enough to get his money's worth. And he had to pee so fucking bad it hurt.

"You're the one with the money, honey."

That he was.

He slid off his stool and took a second to make sure that his legs were going to hold him up. Dallas offered him a hand, but he waved him off. "I got it. I'll be right back."

"I'll follow you. We're headed that way anyhow."

"Suit yourself."

Teague was just drunk enough to wonder why the guy insisted on keeping up the cowboy act when they both knew he was from Jersey. But then, it was probably one of the job requirements. That was kind of funny, being required to act like you were from some ranch in Texas or a horse farm in Tennessee. Still, the guy wasn't entirely wearing a costume. Those were one hundred percent leather boots. They must have cost him four hundred dollars or more. His hat wasn't plastic either. Dallas must be committed to the job, which Teague supposed was admirable.

The man was still basically a stripper, though. A higher-class stripper maybe, but why would anyone make such a big investment in that kind of work? The job didn't exactly involve method acting, and it wasn't so much about what the dancer had *on* as how good he looked once he took it off, right?

"Whoa. Hang on, Wall Street, you passed it."

"Huh?"

"The loo. It's back yonder." The cowboy pointed in the direction they'd come.

"Back yonder, huh?"

"Uh-huh." Jersey cowboy winked at him.

"Thanks." Jesus, Teague had to pee and his head was all muzzy. He turned around and shouldered through the men's room door, nearly taking out a couple that was making out right there in the middle of everything.

Teague grinned. They looked great together. "Excuse me, gentlemen."

The pair didn't even acknowledge his existence, or the existence of anyone else that was coming and going in the busy men's room for that matter. He peed for an age, and they just kept at it. He looked at them in the mirror as he washed his hands and fixed his hair, watched them kissing and touching—nothing X-rated, they were just really into each other—and he wondered what it was like to be them. That kiss was more than "Hey, I just met you on the dance floor, let's make out." No, that kiss was like, "Hey, I'm having a great time, baby, thanks for bringing me and buying me that drink, you're hot when you're dancing."

One of them caught him looking and smiled, and he didn't even blush. He just smiled back. "Looking good, boys," he said as he made his way out to the bar.

"Hey! Wall Street! Didn't we have a date?"

Teague stopped and looked at the cowboy. *Oh. Right.* "Sorry." If he was actually as toasted as he thought he was, this could very well be a waste of good money.

"Come on, darlin', I'm fixin' to make your night."

Teague was ready for that, for sure. Dallas threaded an arm through his, led him along a dimly lit hallway and into a small, private room. Teague happily let the dancer drive. He let Dallas take his jacket, sit him down, undo a couple of buttons more on his dress shirt. He let Dallas run warm hands over his shoulders and man, did that feel good.

"You know the rules, right? No touching unless I put your hands on me, no touching yourself at all, and remember, we're being watched." Dallas pointed to a surveillance camera hanging from the ceiling in one corner and to a long, thin, mirrored window that ran the length of the room. "They'll haul you right out of here if you're not a good boy."

"I'm a good boy." He knew the rules. "Not my first rodeo."

"Oh! Now listen to you with the cowboy talk." Dallas looked at him expectantly. "You're gonna have to take out your billfold, Wall Street."

"Oh." Right. Money. Teague pulled out his wallet and handed over the cash. "Sorry."

"You're doing just fine. You got a song in mind, hon?"

Teague just shook his head. "Nope. Ladies' choice."

"Ha! I ain't no lady. I can promise you that, sugar."

"Bring it on." Avenstone was a mere annoyance now, lingering vaguely around the edges of emotion, a buzzing at the back of his mind. Teague was hoping Dallas's charms would erase his former client from his mind completely.

The music started, and this time it was something he knew with a great beat. Not that it mattered—he didn't even hear it once Dallas let that plaid shirt slide to the floor.

The next few minutes were a blissful, testosterone-filled blur. Dallas rolled his shoulders, rocked his hips, twerked his ass, and generally gyrated in Teague's lap in some very enticing and energetic ways. The Jersey cowboy didn't speak as he danced, but he hooted and laughed and sang along to the music.

And fuck if all of that didn't light Teague up like the top of the Empire State Building. He shifted in his seat more than once to accommodate his swelling cock and kept his eyes riveted on the muscular, hard-bellied, and sweat-sheened dancer.

Dallas, or whatever his name really was, was fucking beautiful. From those amazing green eyes to his ripped shoulders to his six-pack and then some.

As the song came to an end, Teague pulled out his wallet and handed Dallas a hundred-dollar bill. His rational mind was mercifully and completely disconnected now, allowing him to enjoy his buzz and the pleasant haze of hormones. Twenty, fifty, he didn't give a rat's ass. He just didn't want this cowboy to stop dancing yet.

Dallas took the cash. "You sure, Wall Street?"

"I'm sure. Whatever it costs. The rest is for you."

"Yeehaw." Dallas stepped away, waved the cash at the security camera and another song came on, something loud with a raunchy guitar, and the cowboy slid right out of his cutoffs.

Oh, hello again, black thong.

He wanted a kiss. He wanted to take this beautiful dancer home with him. It wasn't going to happen, and he didn't let himself pretend it was, but he felt like he could picture Dallas in his bed, staring up at him, smiling hotly.

He blinked to clear the image from his mind and focused on the part of this that was real.

The thong looked even better up close. Dallas kept a distance of maybe three feet this time, but he put on a show that would make a sailor blush. Teague wondered what it said about him that he didn't. It definitely had other effects, though, and by the time the song was over, Teague wasn't sure he would be able to stand up to leave without embarrassing himself, and his mouth had gone dry as a desert. Dallas was shameless and into the music. Teague was pretty sure he saw a genuine smile. And it wasn't just the alcohol.

He was just considering his predicament when a bottle of water appeared in his line of vision. "You are *very* drunk, but you look like you enjoyed yourself, Wall Street."

"It's T—" Teague choked on the words, coughed, and opened the bottle of water. "Teague." He tipped the bottle up, swallowing down a big gulp.

"I like Wall Street better." Dallas laughed.

"I work in Midtown." Hadn't he said that already?

"So? I live in Brooklyn and they call me a cowboy." Dallas winked at him.

"That was—" *really fucking hot and you're so beautiful, oh, please come home with me—* "very enjoyable." He wasn't sure he'd ever met anyone so lovely.

Dallas laughed, the sound loud and echoing in the bare-walled room. "Yeah, Wall Street, I can definitely see that." The cowboy raked bright eyes over Teague's partially bared chest and rested a hungry gaze on his groin just long enough to make him sweat.

He swallowed hard. "Damn, I ought to make you pay *me* for that look."

Dallas winked at him. "Not my first ride either, Wall Street."

Teague shook his head and finished his water. Christ, he had better excuse himself before he sprayed his shorts.

"All right—Teague, was it? Time to go, man." Well, well. The cowboy was gone, and Brooklyn was making himself heard loud and clear. "Leon will be happy to pour you something on the house if you tell him I sent you."

Teague was thinking it might actually be time to go home.

Fucking hell, morning came early.

Teague groaned and rolled over, the sunlight blasting through his half-closed shades, threatening to cleave his skull right in two.

Fucking hell, his head hurt.

He pulled his phone off the nightstand and looked at it. Nine thirty? *Jesus*. He'd better get up, right? He was already late to his own firing.

The apartment was chilly, and his toes curled away from the hardwood flooring as he made his way to the bathroom. What the hell had he set the AC to last night? Tundra?

He peed for an age, but he didn't deal with his cotton mouth or even look in the mirror. *No, not yet.* He needed to start coffee first.

Fucking hell, he thought the hardwood floor was cold? The slate tiles in the kitchen were fucking freezing. He stood on his heels, touching as little of the floor as possible as he set up the coffeemaker, then rushed back to the bathroom, stopping along the way to set the thermostat to something reasonable. He turned on the radiant heat in the floor and the heat lamp in the ceiling, then started the water for a long, hot shower. He was a big fan of all of that luxury, and he was pretty sure if he could land another job in the next three months or so, he'd be able to keep it.

He got in the shower, his blood pounding in his ears now to compliment the constant, stabbing hangover-induced pain behind his eyes. He ducked under the water and stood there, letting it run down his body and soothe everything that ached.

This was good. This was that cold light of day people talked about when the stress of an emotional moment fell away and everything became crystal clear. The searing pain in his head was exactly what he needed. It reminded Teague that he was only human. That clients came and went, and money piled up or slipped through his fingers, but either way, he was still very much alive.

He'd go in today, take his lumps and his severance package, and maybe go on vacation somewhere sunny for a week or so, before setting his sights on something new.

By the time he got out of the shower, he was feeling better. His head still hurt, but the pounding in his ears was gone. He padded into the kitchen and poured himself a cup of coffee and took a sip. Strong and black, it was exactly the slap in the face he wanted. Half an hour later he was shaved, dressed, and waiting for the Downtown D train.

Times Square in the morning was such a different place than it was by night. By rush hour the traffic was relentless, but the sidewalks were pretty spotless, the litter from the previous day was gone, the streets wet and cleaned, and nearly everything was still closed. It was almost like a Sunday morning back home—the only things open were diners and coffee shops, newsstands, and the occasional street vendor selling bagels in parchment paper and hot coffee in those Greek-style, blue-and-white paper cups that read "We are happy to serve you."

Teague stopped for one of those coffees but passed on the bagel. Food didn't hold much appeal at the moment; he was afraid it would come right back up. He lingered outside Times Square Tower for a minute or two, steeling himself for whatever shit storm he was headed into. He had no idea; he deliberately hadn't looked at his office email on his phone on the way in. Whatever was going on, he didn't want to read an email about it before he'd found the courage to go inside.

"Yes, sir. No, sir. I'm sorry, sir. I take full responsibility." He practiced the words out loud on the elevator ride because none of them sat easy with him; then he headed inside.

I'm an excellent attorney. I didn't blow the deal; it evaporated. I'm not going to let this derail me. You're making a mistake in firing me. Those words were much more natural to him, but somehow, he didn't think he'd get a chance to say any of them.

The elevator doors opened on his floor and he stepped out, deciding to go with his regular morning routine, even if he was nearly two hours later than usual. He walked past the receptionist, giving her a nod. "Good morning, Sonia."

"Morning, Mr. Whitaker." She smiled at him just like always. So far so good.

"I assume William wants to see me?" William "Bucky" Foster was a managing partner, Regional Partner-In-Charge, and also head of the New York office. He was *the* firm bigwig in the tri-state area.

Sonia shrugged. "Not that I know of. Mr. Foster isn't in yet."

Huh. "Thanks, Sonia."

Teague headed down the hall to his office.

"Morning, Barb."

"Good...morning...?" Barbara replied slowly, drawing out the words until they became the question he knew she wanted to ask. His assistant was anything but subtle.

"Barb. You haven't bothered with polite since the day I hired you, why start now?"

Barb grinned and got up from her desk, following him into his office.

Teague took a deep breath, absurdly relieved to find everything in his office right where he'd left it. His briefcase sat untouched on top of his desk, his chair was neatly pushed in, and there was some interoffice mail in his inbox.

"What happened?"

"Greed, I suppose."

"Well, that's ridiculous. Welcome to M and A."

Teague nodded. Barb was smarter than your average bear. When he'd hired her, she was on the back end of raising three boys and was re-entering the workforce with a paralegal certification and no experience. She'd taken the job, closed her mouth and opened her ears, and now, four years later, she could talk the talk with any attorney in Transactions. "Yes. And welcome to young, brilliant, arrogant, socially stunted researchers that are saving lives one dollar at a time."

"Ouch."

That wasn't fair and he knew it; he was just hungover and feeling bitter. "Sorry. I might be feeling a little defensive this morning." He swallowed down the last of his coffee and stared at the empty cup. *Damn.* That was fast.

These brilliant young people had worked their asses off to create a tiny robotic heart valve that could very well revolutionize the field of cardiac medicine one day. One day soon, even. And they'd done it while living on coffee, ramen noodles, and three hours of sleep a night, never sure they'd have enough funding from week to week to finish the job. They deserved every dollar their time, expertise, and devotion were worth. To Avenstone, or to anyone. If they thought they could get a better offer, then good for them.

"Coffee?"

Teague looked at her. "In all the time you've been working with me, I have never once asked you to get me coffee. But thank you."

"You didn't ask, I offered. As a human being that can see you're hungover and hurting. And you really are defensive, aren't you?"

"Jesus." Teague sighed. "I'm sorry, Barb."

"I'm getting you coffee. Sit. Check your email. Or don't and stare out the window. You need an attitude adjustment."

That was for sure. Teague decided to do what he was told and sat down at his desk.

After turning on his computer and pulling up Outlook, he skimmed the firm-wide emails and answered some easy ones regarding the two other deals he was supporting for one of the partners. He ignored a couple of requests for meetings and other scheduling stuff.

He also avoided the email from Kent Orsi at Avenstone.

Barb came back with a tall coffee, a bottle of water, and two Tylenol.

"You are the best, Barb. I appreciate it."

"I'd have lost my temper yesterday. I was impressed with how cool you played everything."

"There honestly wasn't anything to lose my temper about. Avenstone was disappointed, the sellers want what they feel they are entitled to, and there just wasn't a compromise. Not with what we already had in place." It was frustrating, but he wasn't angry. And even if he had been, it would have done him zero good to lose it. It would only have made things worse.

"I have an email from Orsi."

Barb nodded. "Take the Tylenol."

"Right." He did.

"Okay, I'll leave you to it. Shout if you need me." Barb left his office, closing his door behind her.

He stared at the email for a long while, sipping his coffee. He hadn't the foggiest idea what Kent could possibly want with him today, other than maybe to ask for his files back. He was about to click on it when another email came in—a reply to the first—from William. He blinked at it a couple of times and a response to William's reply came in from Kent. Teague sighed. Okay, this was active, and William was on it. He needed to step up.

He opened the first email, the one from Kent, and read it slowly. He lifted his fingers to his aching forehead and rubbed in a slow circle. His hangover must be worse than he thought.

He read it again, and his heart started pounding.

The third time, he read it standing up, shifting from foot to foot and tapping his fingers on the desktop.

Bucky,

I've had a phone call from the sellers. David Rasner sent me the bones of a new proposal with alternate terms, and we think it's worth considering. We'd like to negotiate.

We can't do it without Whitaker. I hope he's still available.

Best regards,

Kent

Teague clicked on the reply from William.

I'm sure he'd be happy to continue his work with you. Lunch Monday?

Bucky

That was the understatement of the century. The final email from Kent read,

Made res, 12:30, Steinberg's Steakhouse, 46th b/n 5th & Madison. Does that work for you, Teague?

K.

Does that work for him? Shit, a fucking cheeseburger from Micky D's and a vanilla shake would work for him if it meant keeping his damn job.

He leaned over the keyboard and replied.

Great news. Sounds perfect. Ready to get to work.

Teague

So ready.

"Barb," he shouted.

It took her about half a second to come through his door. "Twelve thirty on Monday. Steinberg's?"

"How—"

"Mr. Orsi's secretary emailed me."

"I'll need—"

"A car for you and Mr. Foster. On it."

"And will you please ask Kent's secretary for the email string to and from the seller and any attached documents?"

"Sure. I'll get that to you ASAP."

"Barb." He grinned, relief settling deep and starting to unravel the knot in the pit of his stomach. "I am so not fired."

Barb smiled at him. "Not today."

"I'll take it."

"Calls to make." Barb left his office, leaving the door open this time.

Jesus Christ, what a fucking roller coaster this transactions business could be. He could hardly believe he'd been handed another chance to nail this. He'd sell his soul to make it happen.

We can't do it without Whitaker.

He might frame that fucking email and put it on the wall for the next time his ass was on the line. Shit, he'd been so sure that bridge was out for good, but here was Avenstone telling the managing partner that he was indispensable.

Teague flopped back into his chair with a sigh, tired but happy. Proud, even. God, to think he'd been such a mess last night. Just...wrecked. He thought about that lovely dancer who'd helped him forget his troubles. It didn't matter that he'd been drunk; Teague remembered everything about those eyes, that thong, the way his body lit up as Dallas danced for him. He couldn't forget that magnetism either, how real it had felt. He'd finally relaxed, let the stress go. And he'd never forget the way Dallas's eyes took him in like his suit was invisible.

There was a casual rap on his door and he coughed and sat up, clearing thoughts of the dancer from his mind. He was at work. Right. He looked up to find Carson leaning in his doorway.

"Heard the Avenstone deal's been resuscitated."

Damn, news traveled fast. Teague nodded, going with the metaphor. "Apparently the seller gave it mouth-to-mouth last night."

"Let's do lunch today. Noon. Don't turn me down this time, it's on me."

He looked at his watch. "That's in fifteen minutes."

"Yep. No time to make up an excuse not to go." Carson laughed. "Meet you at the elevator."

"You got it." No wasn't an option, apparently. He'd manage. He even thought maybe he might have his appetite back.

Teague sank into his chair and looked around his office. His eyes skimmed the diplomas hanging on the wall: his BS from Harvard and his JD from NYU. He looked over the mahogany bookcase and credenza that held his reference books as well as a few pictures and mementos from various outings he'd been on with clients of the firm, ran his fingers along the length of his desktop, and finally drew a finger across his phone and dialed Barb.

"Hey."

"Hey, can you block out lunch for me? Carson's not taking no for an answer."

"Not to worry, he's way ahead of you," she said dryly.

Teague chuckled. "Of course he did. Thanks, Barb."

He decided to read over the email string he'd asked Barb to send him before lunch and found it enlightening.

Lunch was enlightening, too.

"So what brought them back to the table?" Carson picked up his glass of sparkling water.

"The seller is going with a new law firm."

"No shit. Seriously?"

"Truth. They fired the firm I'd been in negotiations with and hired a new one. They requested a few days to get their new representation up to speed, and then presumably we'll be back at the table."

Teague had been convinced that Avenstone had gone over his head to William to get him fired when, in fact, they had been explaining that he wasn't to blame, that the collapse of the deal was essentially all about the selling party's dissatisfaction with their representation.

Carson nodded. "Crazy. I guess they weren't happy about losing Avenstone either."

"They can't have been. There was a lot of money on the table. I get the feeling they're looking for a different kind of deal, and I think they're making a good decision. Avenstone isn't a venture firm; they have reason to be interested in acquiring these guys. I think their former firm was looking at the deal all wrong."

"Huh. Well, good luck, man."

"Thanks." He took a bite of the sliced seared tuna that was on his salad. "This is delicious. Thanks for treating, you didn't have to do that."

"You should have let me take you out last night. You know I'd have improved your mood."

Teague sighed and shook his head, keeping his eyes on his salad. "It always comes back to that for you, doesn't it?"

"Come on, man. You should give us another shot."

Us? What?

"We've been over this. We work together, and I'm trying to make partner." Teague was sorry he'd allowed anything to happen in the first place, let alone a second time. Fucking office parties.

Carson was told he was close to partner a couple of months ago, and now it was more than just stupid for them to get together. It was completely inappropriate given that Carson was about to be in a superior position at the firm. And the guy wasn't even that good in bed. Not that they'd actually been in bed. He wasn't a great lay in Teague's office, the elevator, or on Carson's couch. At least that was what Teague was telling himself to stay out of trouble.

Teague had never had a single drink at any office function since.

Carson sighed. "Let's go out tonight, Teague."

"Carson."

"Come on, a drink, a good time, why the hell not? It's not like I'm going to tell anyone. And even if they found out, the first time we got together was before I knew about this partner thing, so they can't call it *quid pro quo*."

"Oh, yeah? Since when are you a white-collar employment attorney?"

"Shut up. Drinking, dancing, no pressure after that. Just some like-minded company to help you blow off some steam. You're wound up so tight I could flick my finger at you and snap you in half."

Wrong. He wasn't wound up at all. He'd just had his job saved by the same people he was sure were trying to have his ass. He was cool as a cucumber. He rolled his neck to the side and rubbed one of his shoulders, feeling his upper back crack. So, okay, he was a little stiff. That was age, not tension. It was tough being thirty.

Four.

He was thirty-four.

Damn it.

"Fine. I know a club."

"Text it to me and I'll be there."

5

Those boots were worth every hard-earned dollar Jason had spent on them. Everything about him hurt this morning except his feet. He'd shimmied and gyrated and ground his hips last night and brought home his rent for next month, but today he felt like he was a thousand years old.

He'd hauled himself onto the subway as soon as he got out of bed. He wished he could get a better rate for a gym in Brooklyn, but all the cheaper monthly deals were at the chain gyms in the city. A hike, but he made it work. He wondered if it was time to switch up his gym routine. He spent so much time dancing now, maybe he didn't need five days a week. He finished his run, shut the treadmill off, and found a good spot to stretch out. He sucked down half a bottle of water and walked in a circle to cool off a bit more; then he bent at the waist to try to touch his toes. He ended up just hanging there for a bit, feeling some of the tightness in his hips release and his back open up. Finally. God, that felt good.

"Putting on a nice little show." A hand connected with his ass with a solid *thud*.

Danny.

"Howdy, sugar." Jason stood up, feeling a little lightheaded for a second.

"Don't 'howdy' me when you're not in your little straw hat, *Crooklyn*."

"Shit." Jason snorted, he hadn't even realized he'd done it. Dude. "Sorry, man. What's good?" He put his hand on the wall and stretched his quads.

Danny shrugged. "Same old workout, different day."

"I hear that." The gym felt different to him now that being in great shape was a job requirement and not just a hobby. He still loved it, but part of it felt like work these days. "Whatdya got left?"

"I'm done, baby. I was just about to hit the showers."

"I've got a circuit with the free weights, can you give me fifteen? We could get some lunch."

"Sounds great. I'll make it a long shower." Danny winked at him and sauntered off, hips swinging. Jason laughed and got to it.

His shower was long-ish too. Maybe he needed to spring for a massage once a week. He was hurting today. At first, he pretended not to notice that Danny was watching him towel off and dress with much more interest than was typically acceptable in a locker room. But when he met Danny's gaze and the man smiled at him, he had to call Danny out.

"Yo. What are you looking at?"

"Mm. You. So pretty with all your muscles."

"Thanks. I guess." Jason laughed. Danny was as shameless as he was.

He finished dressing, tamed his dirty-blond mop into submission with a comb and a little product; then he followed Danny out. Lunch was Thai and Danny ate like the bird he was. Jason, though, ordered half the menu.

"Going out to eat with you is always such an event." Danny picked up his tea and leaned back in his chair. "I don't know why I bother to order anything, I could just pick off your plate and you'd never notice."

That was probably true. Jason snorted. "I work hard."

"You do. Aaron thanked me the other night."

"For?"

"Bringing you in. He likes you. He says the guests like you."

Guests. That was what Aaron called the people that came to the bar. Not customers or patrons. Guests. Like the place was Disney World. Jason thought that was odd, but he wasn't going to argue with the man that signed his paycheck.

"That's good to know, I guess. I like the job, it's fun, I get to play some and, well, the *men*."

"Everywhere you look." Danny's grin took over his whole face. "Heaven."

"I'm sore as hell, though. Does that get better?"

"A little. I get a massage once a week; that's really helpful. Not cheap, but the first time you try to work with your back spasming, and you somehow have to make it through the night anyway? You'll realize the investment is worth it."

"Oh, I was just thinking about that. It sounds like a great idea." That was probably a good point. If he was this sore today and worked tonight, how was he going to feel tomorrow? "Can I get the name of your guy?"

Danny pulled out his phone. "It's a woman, but she's got hands that will turn you to jelly."

"Fine by me."

"I just texted you her deets."

"Thank you."

Danny peered at him over a glass of water. "So, how is Brooklyn?"

"You're asking about the roomies? Fine."

"Lee and...the linebacker guy?"

"Shamus." Shamus's shoulders were as wide as two of Danny.

"They're good?"

"Yep. They're great..." He had a feeling he knew where this conversation was going.

"And Ricky? Is he still bartending?"

Uh-huh. That was subtle. How adorable. "Yep. He's at, uh—" Which one was it? "O'Donohue's? O'Halloran's? O'Doyle's? Some Irish pub."

Danny wrinkled his nose. "That is not helpful, honey." Ricky and Danny had hit it off when the roomies took Ricky out for his birthday a couple of weeks ago. Ricky had been asking questions since then, too.

"Sorry." Jason grinned.

"How am I supposed to accidentally walk in and sit at the bar on a night he just happens to be working if I don't know which bar?"

Jason laughed and pulled out his phone.

Yo. Where you working at? he texted.

Ricky replied in seconds. His fingers must have been on fire. *McAlstead's Pub. Amsterdam/81st. Is my boy Danny asking? Tell him I'll have a drink waiting.*

"Oh, he's way the fuck uptown now. Eighty-first Street."

"Whoa. East side or west?"

"West, on Amsterdam. And the pub's not an O'something—it's a Mc'something."

Danny leaned forward. "Are you going to tell me or just stare at your phone?"

Jason grinned and looked up at Danny. "He's so on to you."

"Oh." Danny looked thoughtful for a minute. "Well, that's okay. That means he's been thinking about me. Right? Tell me where."

"Yup. Texting it to you so you'll have it."

Danny looked at his phone and smiled as Jason's text came in. "Yeah, Eighty-first? I better clean my place; I can't send him all the way home to Brooklyn from Eighty-first Street late at night after a date."

"Never. So kind of you to think of him." Jason winked and went back to his lunch.

Even Danny couldn't keep a straight face. "Such a commute, the poor darling."

"You two might actually be good together."

Danny's sarcastic grin softened into a smile. "You think?" He bit his lip.

"I do. Ricky's fun. And sincere. He's kind of a slut, though, so be warned. I mean, he can commit, I think, but he'll never stop flirting."

"I'm good with that as long as he can handle a little of his own medicine. I mean. Look where we work, right? Flirting is half the job." Danny winked.

Jason nodded, smiling and happy to see both of his friends starting something new. "I guess we'll see, won't we?"

The table got quiet for a minute or so while they both ate. The longer the silence went on, though, the more Jason was sure what was on Danny's mind.

"Have you—"

"Nope. Not in weeks. I think he moved to Westchester."

"Just as well."

"Damn right." Jason had once thought he and Simon had a real thing. They'd been together for a year or so when Simon asked him to move in. Jason had spent every dime he'd had to move to Queens because he was convinced it was love. Ricky, Shamus, and Lee had helped him move, and it really had been bliss for a couple of months.

"I still can't believe he hit you."

"Oh, he didn't hit me. If he'd connected, I'd have gone full Jersey City on his French-fried ass. He woulda been moved to Bellevue in an ambo, not upstate in *zee U-Haul, no*?"

Danny laughed. "Damn. Don't mess with Jersey."

Jason winked. "Hell, no."

"So are you seeing any—"

"Nope."

"I might know—"

"Nope." No. He was single and happy.

"Jase."

"Thanks, Danny, but no."

"Hm." Danny sipped his tea. "Well, you're no fun."

"I'm not turning it off, Danny, I'm just going to keep my options open for a bit."

"Okay, baby. If you say so."

God, Jason hated when people did that. "Don't patronize me, Danny, okay?"

"Wow. Look at you, getting all defensive. Does that happen every time someone brings up Simon?"

Jason sighed. *Fuck that French tart, anyway.* "Sorry. I just...let's just say it's a good thing I haven't seen him around. This job finally got me dug out of the financial hole all the moving around got me in. I'm getting people paid back and shit. The whole thing was embarrassing, for one thing, and just..." Humiliating. Heartbreaking. Pretty terrifying, even. How stupid was he that he never saw that coming?

"No one ever judged you, baby. We all thought he was straight up."

It was bad, but his friends had been there when he needed them. That was something he would never forget. He might have been dead broke all that time, but he was rich in friends for sure.

Jason shrugged. He should be over it by now; it wasn't like he'd actually been hurt, not physically, but he just...it got to him. That one action made everything he'd believed about his relationship into a lie in one second flat. He couldn't promise he wouldn't smack his ex-lover down if he ran into Simon again. He hadn't done it at that moment because he'd been so shocked and heartbroken. At the time, all he'd been thinking about was getting out. But by the time he'd gotten home to his old apartment and his roomies got him inside, he'd been so ready to go right out again. Shamus had practically sat on him, and Lee had spent time talking slowly to him like he was a wild-eyed animal. Ricky had brought him tequila.

Thank fuck for Ricky.

"Well, I haven't seen him since I moved in with the guys again, and I don't intend to see him." A Brooklynite had no business in Queens, anyway.

"Sounds good to me, love."

Danny reached around the table and took Jason's hand, giving it a squeeze, and Jason fought back the threat of tears that stung the corners of his eyes. That emotion had nothing to do with Simon and everything to do with Danny being kind to him and giving him some love. Sometimes people caring was tough for him to take.

"I'm thinking something gooey for dessert; will you share it with me?"

"I'm trying to watch my figure, but..." Danny winked.

"Oh, please. You know I'll eat most of it anyway."

Danny smiled at him. "Okay, baby. Bring it on."

6

W hen Teague arrived at The Wiggle Room, Carson was already waiting for him.

Of course.

He took a deep breath before stepping out of his Uber. They'd both had enough time to go home and change and, if he were honest, he had to admit that Carson looked good. Blue jeans that fit just right and a gray short-sleeved V-neck that hugged across a broad chest. *Damn*. Teague really didn't want to be attracted to that guy.

"Look at you, Mister Metro. Are those pants leather?" Carson put an arm around Teague's shoulders. Teague laughed just so he had an excuse to shake Carson off without seeming rude. Maybe later, after a few drinks, maybe then Carson would look like someone he could get off with. Right now, his colleague looked like a very bad idea with a side of "How stupid are you, Teague?"

"Yes. Leather." Carson could tease all he liked, Teague loved them. They were comfortable, and they always looked great on him. Now that he thought about it maybe he should have gone for something less hot, though. "Let's get a drink."

"Wow, see what I'm saying? Someone's wound up."

Teague didn't say anything; he just got into the entry line. Together, they didn't need any help getting in. They paid their cover and headed inside, where Teague made a beeline for the overcrowded bar.

Carson slipped past him and elbowed in, claiming a narrow spot at the bar. "What are you—" Carson raised his voice to be heard over the music. "What are you having?"

"Beer."

"Have a cocktail, man."

Really? "Okay. Whiskey sour."

Carson ordered and looked at him. "What's the matter with you?"

"Nothing. I'm fine. I'm great." That may have sounded sarcastic, but it wasn't. He was great. He was better than great. He just wasn't sure he should be *here*. Not with Carson. They just didn't mesh.

Carson snorted and leaned in. "You need to lighten up."

That.

That right there? That was why he and Carson wouldn't ever—couldn't ever—go further than sex. Carson was just too self-absorbed.

Teague was plenty light, actually. He was elated. To go from last night's low to today's high? Man, he felt like Superman. Hell, he was in his favorite leather at a wild club with hot men he could watch all night without feeling self-conscious. He was surrounded by neon lights and alcohol. He just felt absolutely nothing for the man standing next to him, and knowing himself, they'd end up fooling around later anyway. He was into getting off as much as the next guy, but he was tired of the *with whom* not mattering.

Teague rested one elbow on the bar and looked up at the stage, where a stunning Latino dancer was wiggling his hips off, wearing a very small pair of hot-pink spandex boy shorts that left little to the imagination.

Their drinks arrived, and Teague picked his up and sipped it. Maybe if he didn't get rocked, he could remember to get an Uber home alone. It wasn't likely, but it wasn't impossible, either.

It was seriously crowded at the club tonight, way more than last night. More men, more guys with trays serving drinks, more dancers. There was a second bar open that hadn't been last night, and the music was louder too. Guess that was the difference between Thursday and Friday? *Here's to the weekend.*

"How's your drink?" Carson leaned close. He didn't have much choice, honestly, it was tight at the bar.

"It's good, actually. Really good."

"Good." That seemed to make Carson happy and he gestured to the hot dancer on stage. "He's pretty, huh?"

"Yeah, I was just thinking that. He has a great ass. And those shorts look amazing. Mm-mm."

"You're a little bit of a hound dog, huh?" Carson laughed.

Teague shrugged. "Come on. He knows he looks good, that's the point, right? He knows we're watching, that guys are talking about him. He knows exactly what's up. He's counting on it. If he's not offended, I'm not a hound dog."

"I guess."

"No, definitely. That's how he makes his living. He's hot and he knows it."

Carson shrugged and looked at one of the TVs behind the bar. "Baseball."

Teague glanced over, then back at the stage. "You a little uncomfortable, Carson?" That was an amusing thought.

"What? No."

"Too many hot, half-naked men making you feel inadequate?" Teague laughed.

"Oh, shut up. I can give them a run for their money."

"Well, I suppose you do have a nice ass."

Carson shot him a look. "You can have it, man. Your place or mine?"

"Whoa. Slow that train down, skippy." *Like, leave it at the station, please.*

"You're too much." Carson's eyes were on the TV.

"I see what you're doing. You're changing the subject."

"What?"

"Turn around and watch this lovely man dance with me."

Carson pointed at the TV. "Baseball."

"Turn around, chickenshit."

"What?" Carson turned around. "No need to call names."

Teague looked him up and down. This good-looking man, who clearly had a healthy libido, was embarrassed to watch a beautiful body dance on stage. Talk about repressed. Well, Teague would let Carson squirm a little as long as it was fun, and he wouldn't push the issue if Carson wasn't digging it.

But then the song ended, and that was that. Carson winked at him and went back to his baseball. Teague shook his head, grinning, and took another sip of his drink.

"Gentlemen!" The announcement was loud.

Teague looked at the stage, his head turning automatically.

"Lock up your sons and your horses and give a holler for...Dallas!"

The familiar-but-not strains of a country guitar and a

fired-up fiddle filled the club, and the bright white spotlight caught the cowboy at the other end of the bar, kissing some other unsuspecting, tie-wearing schmuck. Teague smiled, his fingers running reflexively across his lips as he watched. He was surprised by the movement and pulled his fingers away, frowning at them, a little perplexed.

"Yeehaw!"

Teague blinked when Carson hooted, realizing that he'd disappeared there for a second. It seemed like everything had gone silent with that cowboy's kiss, but now, everything sped up again, the hammering beat of the music and the bright club lighting overwhelming him. He put a hand on the bar, needing to touch something solid.

Carson laughed and elbowed him, and Teague stuck a hand out protectively.

"Whoa. You okay, man?"

Teague nodded, feeling stupid now. "Yeah, I'm fine. I guess they're pouring them strong tonight."

Carson snorted. "Lightweight."

Not usually, but damn. He hadn't finished but half his drink. Maybe he was still recovering from his binge the night before—that had been kind of epic, after all. He'd only gotten a few hours' sleep, and he'd been way hung over most of the day. So much for hair of the dog.

The guy next to him left his barstool, and Teague took it. The country song was finally sounding like music again, the fiddle feeling free and easy and the guitar like a hard day's work. Teague watched Dallas dance, watched him work his hips, admired the way he licked his lips and smiled.

He seemed younger than Teague but not by much. And even up there, trying to do his best to give everyone in the room a woody, he seemed...honest. He looked like he was actually enjoying himself.

It really was time to stop drinking.

Dallas was wearing red shorts tonight and they rode obscenely low, even lower than his thong had, showing a lovely light brown trail of hair from just below his navel right on down to where Teague's imagination took over. When he turned his back, he gave everyone an enticing view of the cleft between his muscular ass cheeks with the white waistband, teasing but stopping just so.

Teague was riveted to him until the song ended, and even then, he found himself following the cowboy offstage with his eyes until he was obscured from view by bouncers and other men.

He needed to move. "I'm going to dance."

"Huh?"

Teague looked at Carson. He needed to blow off some steam; that cowboy got him a little hot under the waistband. "Dance. Come on."

Carson tossed back his drink and set the empty glass on the bar. "That's what I'm talking about." Teague led the way and Carson followed, finally grabbing hold of Teague's hand to keep up through the crowd. At least that was what Teague was hoping he was up to.

Teague found a spot where they could have a little air between them. Carson smiled at him and started to move, and Teague joined in, feeling the thump and thud of the bass and drum funnel up through his feet, fill his chest and trickle out to the ends of his fingers. He did like to dance—it was something he easily forgot about, though, because it wasn't much of a priority, and when he did go out to places like this, he usually arrived alone.

Carson moved well, smooth and graceful as a cat, his body an extension of the music. The guy knew it too, knew just how good he looked. He grinned at Teague every now and then, his eyes trying to convince Teague to come closer, to have a taste, to take him home. *Fuck*. He was hot as hell, and that was no lie. With every passing second on the dance floor, Carson was feeling like a really good bad idea.

Teague moved closer and Carson took advantage, slipping a hand around Teague's shoulders.

"Wall Street!"

Teague blinked, his leather just barely grazing Carson's denim.

"Hey. Wall Street," Dallas shouted over the music. "Two nights in a row?"

Dallas was a little flushed, and damn, it was a good look on the Jersey cowboy. It broke the spell Carson had him under, and Teague stepped back and took a deep breath, breaking contact. He didn't meet Carson's eyes, because he was sure their reactions to the interruption were completely opposite. Dallas had perfect fucking timing.

"Later, cowboy." Carson dismissed Dallas with an outstretched hand.

"Hey, Dallas."

Carson looked between them. "You know this guy?"

"We met last night, sugar, but he was all by his lonesome. He didn't tell me he had himself a hot boyfriend." Dallas chimed in, undeterred by Carson's rebuff, and moved in on both of them. "A hot boyfriend."

"Carson isn't my boyfriend." *Let's just make that clear, shall we?*

"No?" Dallas grinned and danced right in between them. "Did you tell your not-boyfriend that I was the best lap dance in the club?"

Carson shot Teague a look. "You got a lap dance last night?"

"I did. I needed a distraction." Teague shrugged. He wasn't ashamed.

"Shit, you really are shameless."

He rolled his eyes. "It's in private, idiot. You ever had one?"

Carson shrugged. "Uh."

"You've never had a lap dance?"

"Oh sugar, let this cowboy show you what you're missin'." Dallas reached out and slid a finger along Carson's jaw, and for a second Teague couldn't breathe.

"What does it cost?"

"It's only money, honey, and I know you're good for it. Come on."

Carson looked around Dallas at Teague. "You seriously did this?"

"Yep. It was awesome."

Dallas frowned at him. "I've heard better recs."

Teague shook his head and laughed. "Sorry, Jersey." He looked at Carson. "I couldn't walk. I nearly creamed my tighty-whities. No lie."

"Oh, that's much better, darlin'." Dallas gave him a wink.

Carson raised an eyebrow. "Damn."

Teague pulled out his wallet. "Here. It's on me." He held out a twenty-dollar bill for Dallas to take.

"Oh. You don't. I mean…"

"Slide it right here, sugar." Dallas stuck out his ass and patted his back pocket.

The first thing Teague did was look around for the bouncers, and Dallas just laughed. "No trouble, Wall Street. My invitation." He patted his ass again.

Teague's fingers started to sweat. He reached out and put the bill into the cowboy's pocket as chastely as he could manage and pulled his hand away quickly.

"Aw, you're a sweetheart. Next time you can cop a feel, Wall Street. I promise."

Teague swallowed. Hard.

"I'll bring him back soon." Dallas took Carson by the arm, and the pair of them disappeared into the mass of gyrating bodies.

"No rush." Teague said to the air. He watched them go, feeling...a little jealous?

Fuck this. He didn't know what the hell was the matter with him. He needed another drink. He wiggled his way out of the crowd, bumping into bodies, getting a mix of smiles and annoyed looks, and finally elbowed in at the bar and ordered a beer.

Looking around he saw a mix of people, almost entirely men, who seemed like they were from pretty much everywhere. White shirts and loose ties, blue jeans and old T-shirts, sleek, all-black types both with and without attitude, regular guys in khakis and button-downs, and the occasional spandex and heels.

Two of those regular guys were next to him, friends probably, tourists for sure, having a conversation and laughing with easy smiles on their faces. A pair of blue-jeans types were leaning on the bar and on each other so close it was hard to tell which was holding the other up. There was a sweet threesome on the dance floor maybe ten feet away, two bigger guys with a smaller, adorable hottie between them.

God, it was hard enough to find one lover; he'd never even hope to find two.

He probably shouldn't hope to find one right now, not in his line of work. There was no time. Especially not with this reborn deal on the table in front of him.

He thought about the couple from last night in the men's

room. If he told Carson that was what he wanted, Carson would probably laugh himself stupid. But Teague knew who he was, and he didn't think being aggressive in the bedroom meant he couldn't find someone to share something totally the opposite outside it.

He finished one beer and was into his second when Carson resurfaced. The man looked a little mussed, quite pink in the cheeks, and he had a satisfied smile on his face.

"Have fun?"

Carson grinned, looking a little sheepish. That look was adorable on him and made Teague tilt his head thoughtfully. Carson looked like something he could get into right now.

Damn. Why didn't I want to take you home again? Oh, God. Fucking beer.

Dallas slid right up next to him. "Your turn, honey?"

Teague shook his head no. "I don't think—"

"Let's go, Wall Street." Dallas leaned a little closer. "We had such a good time last night."

Teague shivered, feeling the goose bumps rise on his arms.

"Go on, man. I'm gonna get a drink." Carson raised a finger to get the attention of a bartender.

"I think I'm good." He didn't trust himself, honestly.

But Carson waved cash at Dallas. "Payback is a bitch." He grinned.

Dallas took the money and put it into his pocket and slipped his hand in Teague's, giving Teague a tug.

Dallas's fingers were warm and seemed to fit just right in his palm, and he suddenly had no interest in arguing anymore. He slid right off the barstool and followed Dallas away from the bar.

They made their way back and ended up in the room

next door to the one they'd been in the night before. The room was warm and smelled like sweat and men. "Busy night?"

"You could say that." Dallas waved at the security camera. He put his hands on Teague's shoulders and pushed him down onto a long couch against the wall.

"If you add another twenty, I can ditch the shorts, sugar."

Teague took out his wallet. "You can keep them on." He pressed a fifty into Dallas's palm anyway, and Dallas looked at him, his green eyes bright and warm. "Just keep it."

"Oh." Dallas seemed to freeze for a minute as they looked at each other. "Th-thank you. Maybe you've bought yourself a kiss instead."

"I'd like that." *Please. Please kiss me.*

"No touching, remember. Anything."

Teague caught himself leaning closer. "Unless you put my hands on you."

"Unless...that." Dallas nodded slowly and Teague watched him swallow with interest. "Right."

Jesus Christ, they hadn't taken their eyes off each other, it was a thousand degrees in here, and he was having trouble getting a breath again.

"Okay, shall we do this?" Dallas pushed away suddenly and gave the camera another wave. When the music started up it was loud and nicely balanced, sound surrounding them both. Dallas must have noticed him perk up.

"Yeah, surround sound in here. Nice, huh?" Dallas started to move, stepping close again until he was rocking his hips over Teague's knees.

Teague caught one of his hands starting to reach and he crossed his arms over his chest to keep them still. The longer the song went on, the more Teague tuned it out. He wasn't interested in the music; he was watching the cowboy's face, memorizing Dallas's expression, pale skin, and freckles. He noted that the one freckle just under Dallas's right eye was bigger than most of the others and a little darker, too.

Dallas shifted so his knees were on the couch and he was straddling Teague. He was just barely sitting on Teague's thighs, the weight light and warm, and as soon as their eyes met again, Dallas leaned in and kissed him. It was gentle and sweet, chaste and much too brief.

But it felt like *everything*.

Something shifted inside him, something necessary and deep in the center of Teague's soul. He gasped as Dallas pulled away.

Teague tightened his arms to his chest. Partly to keep from reaching out to pull this man closer and partly to try and ease the ache that had just settled there.

His cry was muffled against Dallas's lips as the cowboy suddenly kissed him again, longer this time. Dallas's lips parted and his tongue darted out, drawing a wet line across Teague's lower lip. Teague experimented, tentatively offering his tongue in return, not wanting to overstep. He was rewarded with a short, desperate sound as Dallas opened up to let him in.

The kiss was nothing like any Teague had experienced before. There was heat, but not the usual rush. Plenty of desire, but more in the moment than pushing toward anything further. Teague assumed that was all Dallas's doing—going any further would break the rules after all, and Dallas wouldn't want to anyway. Whatever was going on in his own mind, in his body, this was just another night's work for the cowboy.

Man, it sure was fun, though.

Dallas pulled away again as the song ended and his eyes

seemed even brighter now as they locked on Teague's for a long, still moment. Teague had no idea how long they stayed like that, and he was just as flustered as Dallas when the lights flashed on and off several times.

Dallas hopped off his lap in a hurry. "Wow. Uh. Hey, glad you decided to come on back tonight."

Teague nodded. "Me too." He was impressed that his voice didn't crack.

"So, yeah. Thanks for the tip, and enjoy your night."

Teague wasn't ready to leave the room just yet, so he took his time straightening his shirt and adjusting his leather, interested to discover he was only half-hard. He looked up as he finished. "What's your real name?"

None of his business but he couldn't stop himself from asking.

"It's—" Dallas stopped speaking abruptly, eyes wide, and the Jersey boy took over like he had last night. "It's time for you to go, man. Have a beer on me."

"Right. I'm sorry. I—" Teague was mortified and headed for the door. Fuck, what was the matter with him? "Really sorry." He rushed out toward the bar but ducked into the men's room instead. Christ, he needed to pull it together. Etiquette. You didn't ask personal questions; the whole lap dance thing was all about the illusion of intimacy. A fantasy. And he'd had himself believing that kiss had been more than a fifty-dollar good time. *Shit*. He splashed cold water on his face and dried off, trying to remember if he'd ever been kissed like that before. He decided it had to be the beer, the hangover, the lack of sleep—pretty much anything but what it actually felt like.

He took another minute to hit the head and wash up, then headed back out to find Carson at the bar.

7

Jason hung out in the dressing room barefoot, wearing some awesome lime-green boxer briefs and flipping through a yuppie men's style magazine—for the men, not the clothing. He didn't give a crap about style, but he could look at the pretty boys all damn day long.

He was way early for work because he woke up this morning to the beginning of a heat wave, and he and his roomies had agreed at the beginning of the summer that they couldn't afford to run the air conditioners. It was one of those city days where the air quality index was hanging out in the red zone, and the mayor was on TV telling everyone who wasn't super healthy to stay indoors or find a cooling center: people with heart problems, lung issues, old people, kids and babies, that kind of thing.

So, it was melt into goo in Brooklyn, hang out in one of the public libraries, or come here. At least here he could get comfy. Weird that it was so hot in September, but it happened sometimes. The sun was so strong his cheap flip-flops were trying to melt into the sidewalk on the way over.

And this was the beginning of a three- or four-day run of ninety-plus weather. God.

Jason wasn't alone. There were a few other dancers hanging out, too; Hulk was stretched out on the couch, sound asleep and snoring softly. He was huge, as his dancer name implied, though they didn't paint him green, thank God. His real name was Jeffrey, he lived in Alphabet City someplace with his girlfriend, and also Sam and Sam's boyfriend. Sam went by Damien and wore little devil horns and a sequined tail. Sam was here, too, somewhere, doing pushups in the hall or something.

Jackson had come through a little while ago, and he and Jesse had disappeared together. It didn't take a genius to figure out what that was about. And Emilio—which was a stage name, but Emilio used it exclusively at the club—was sitting cross-legged on the floor, listening to music and writing in a journal. Jason could hear the quiet tinny sound of the music leaking around Emilio's headphones.

Danny had texted to say he was on his way, but the subways were moving as slowly as everyone else was today.

Aaron stuck his head into the room. "Dallas," he barked, pointing at Jason. "My office."

Jason watched him disappear again and cringed. He'd kind of hoped that weird thing with Mr. Wall Street Friday night had flown under the radar, but maybe not. He still wasn't sure what had happened; he'd just gotten lost for a minute. He'd tried to push thoughts of their kiss out of his head all weekend, but it wasn't easy. Wall Street was definitely still on his radar.

He put his magazine down, slid off the dressing-room chair, and padded out into the hall toward Aaron's office in his still-bare feet. He took a few deep breaths, determined not to lose his job over something so short-lived and stupid. Aaron was usually cool about stuff—he figured at worst he'd get a warning and maybe a little slap on the wrist.

He stepped into Aaron's office.

" 'Sup, boss?"

"Close the door, Jason." Aaron usually called everyone by their stage names, to be respectful of those guys who didn't want their real names out there. Like Emilio. Emilio only danced once in a while for extra money. He did something else for work, but Jason didn't know what it was and he sure wasn't going to ask.

So it didn't seem like a great omen that Aaron was using his real name. Jason reached behind him and closed the door, then plopped in a chair opposite Aaron's desk. "So what—"

"Jason you had a visitor a few minutes ago."

Oh, shit. A "visitor" sounded a little freaky. Had Simon found him? His heart started to pump a little harder. "Uh. Okay. I wasn't expecting anyone."

"Asshole lawyer. Sharp suit. Expensive shoes." Aaron slapped a business card on the desk. "He left that. He wanted you to know he was looking for you."

Jason reached for the card.

"That is some big-time legal outfit in Times Square."

"A lawyer?" He looked down at the card. "Teague Whitaker."

"Name familiar?"

"Uh...no?" Wall Street. It was Irish. It wasn't a name he'd easily forget. Teague was here a few minutes ago? *Shit.* "Nope."

Aaron leaned forward on his desk. "I told that prick to fuck off. This time. But that's all I can do for you, man, you got that? He comes around with a cop or a warrant or some fucking thing I'm gonna have to play along. And your ass will be fired on the spot. *Finito.* You feel me?"

Jason stared at the card, their kiss coming back to him in a rush. He felt his cheeks heat. "I—yes. I feel him. *You.* I feel —" *Oh, my God.* "I got it."

"Unless your rich uncle died and left you money or you're testifying against a fucking serial killer or some shit, I don't want to know dick. I don't want to see anything, I don't want any part of your fucking circus. Am I very, *very*, crystal fucking clear, Jason?"

"Yes, sir. Crystal clear. He won't come around again. I promise." *Jesus Christ.*

Aaron stared at him for a long moment, eyes narrow, brow furrowed. It felt like Aaron was trying to see into his soul. Or deeper, all the way back to his fucking childhood or something. Jason returned the look. If there was one thing he knew for sure, that blueblood Wall Street suit wasn't going to lose him his job, no matter how hot he was.

No matter how unforgettable that kiss.

No matter how much Jason would give to see him again.

"All right. We're good, then. I'm going to forget he came by, and you're going to make sure I don't see that flashy suit again, and we'll call it handled."

"Yes, sir. I'm on it." He got up and headed for the door.

"You know, you're kicking ass out there, Dallas. I had my doubts—you seemed a little soft, but you're killing it."

"Thank you, sir. I appreciate the work."

Aaron grinned. "I can see that. Keep it up, you never know when an opportunity might come up."

Jason nodded. "Yes, sir. Thank you, sir."

"You can go relax. Leave the door open."

"Right. Thanks. Uh. Right." Jason left the office and headed back toward the dressing room. He stopped just outside the door and looked at the business card. Wall Street had only said his name once and it was over the music, but Jason knew. He *knew*. This was definitely the guy. He started to smile, remembering the taste of whiskey sour and sweat on the guy's lips and the sweet, slow, sensual connection in that kiss. God, how he wanted more of that.

But a man like Wall Street didn't want someone like Jason. He couldn't possibly. It was the *idea* of Jason that Wall Street wanted. The fantasy of a private dancer in his bedroom. A cowboy.

Jason sobered and grabbed his phone off the dressing table. Realizing he wasn't going to be able to make a private call here, he slipped on a tank top, shorts, and his flip-flops and headed outside. The air that hit him felt like he'd opened the door to a furnace. A hot wind blew into his face and through his hair and he closed the door behind him quickly, so he didn't let the fucking fiery depths of Hell inside. He climbed up the steps and under the marquee, where at least there was some shade.

This guy was stupidly reachable. The business card had a website, email, general office line, direct line, fax—but the cell phone number had a star next to it, so he picked that one. It rang exactly once.

"Whitaker."

"Wall Street?"

"Uh. Hey. Dallas? Hi." Jason heard a door close.

"So, my boss told me you stopped by and left me your card."

"Oh, good. I mean, obviously. Or you wouldn't be calling me. I wasn't sure he would. I mean, he seemed kind of pissed. Told me off and slammed the door."

"Yeah? Shocker."

"What?"

He took a deep breath and went on. "Listen up, asshole. I don't guess you have any idea that you almost cost me my job."

"I—"

"You're a fucking lawyer and you show up at my job looking for me, not saying why, saying you need to speak with me?"

"Well, that was just so he'd—"

"And he did. But you listen up. Don't come here again. Not like that. I've been warned, and I need this fucking job. You come around like that again and you won't have to worry about the bouncers, I will kick your ass myself. You want to play out your pretty little cowboy fantasy, you can show up at the front door and pay a cover like everyone else."

The line went silent and stayed silent. Jason pulled the phone away from his ear and looked at it. The call was still connected. He put it back to his ear, only now realizing that he'd worked himself into a sweat. He leaned against a concrete wall, hoping it would be cool, but it wasn't. It was solid, though, and he stayed there, waiting.

"You there or what?"

"You're not a cowboy," Whitaker said finally.

"What?"

"I don't have any cowboy fantasies. You're not a cowboy. You're a dancer from Jersey."

"Brooklyn."

"Fine. But not Texas."

Jason's heart started to pound for real. "Yeah. That's...right."

Teague's voice dropped low. "You wanted to tell me your name. I know you did."

"Wall Street, I—"

"It's Teague."

"Sorry." He sighed. He wasn't sure he liked the turn the conversation was taking.

"What's your name?"

Shit. He was right. "I'm not supposed to...I mean how do I know you're not, like, a pervert or something?"

"I gave Dallas fifty dollars Friday night."

"Huh?"

"I paid Dallas fifty dollars. But I couldn't buy a kiss like that for fifty thousand."

Jason gasped, and his chest started to burn as if he were going to burst into flames. He was very glad he was already leaning against a wall, because his knees weren't feeling so steady now either. He tried to talk himself down. There was no way this guy actually meant those words, right? Like, for real? Sure, the guy might believe it now, but Teague had a little fantasy crush on Dallas the cowboy. Something brought on by testosterone, alcohol, and the haze of artificial fog and stage lighting.

"Tell me I'm wrong." Oh, that voice sounded so strong, so confident.

"What?"

"Tell me that was a throwaway kiss, and you were just tossing a hook at me, looking for tips. Tell me you felt nothing at all, that you didn't want more. Tell me you didn't see something you need in my eyes. Come on, Jersey, say it. Tell me that—or tell me your name."

Jason was so frustrated, so torn, that tears welled up and spilled right out of him. They rolled over his cheeks as he paced, not knowing what he should do. Of course it was more than a kiss. Who was he kidding? Wall Street— *Teague's* eyes were so blue, light blue like the water in those pictures of faraway places with white sand beaches. And they were just as clear, too; Jason could swear he saw all the way to the bottom.

But.

"No." Jason protested, embarrassed that he couldn't keep the emotion out of his voice, but it was what it was. "No, I can't unless I...you have to meet me. I need to see you. Tomorrow night. You show up, you tell me what you just told me now but in person, and I'll decide. I can't just—not over the phone."

"Okay." There was a sigh on the other end of the line. "Okay, yeah, I get that. When and where?"

"Johnny's at seven." He was really doing this. *Shit.*

"In the village, right? I'll be there."

"See you then."

"I'm looking forward to it. You're going to want to tell me your real name, Jersey cowboy. I swear you will. I'm completely sincere."

Jason swiped at his eyes. He already wanted to, but he didn't trust that feeling right now. "Good night." He hung up before he could say anything else.

8

Teague had hung out with Carson for another hour or so at the bar Friday night, but only because Carson was into the game on TV and wasn't talking much. He'd ordered one more whiskey sour and sipped it slowly, staring down at the bar and worrying the edge of a cocktail napkin. Over and over he'd played that kiss on repeat in his mind, obsessed. It was supposed to have been staged, but it wasn't. It was supposed to have been nothing, just a reward for a nice tip, but it had been much more than that. It had been incomprehensible. Transcendent. Like the slow burn of an oil lamp, the flame steady and bright. And Teague was sure it had been just as startling for Dallas; he'd seen it in the dancer's eyes.

Once he'd come to that conclusion, he'd called himself an Uber, made his excuses to Carson, and headed right the fuck home to pace for an hour and sober up. But even sober and sleepless, even in the light of the dawn, even after his first few sips of strong, black coffee, nothing so insane had ever felt so right to him before. It had taken him all weekend to get up the courage to drop off that business card. He wasn't someone to just put himself out there and wait for them to either call or not.

The call came quickly, and it wasn't exactly the one he'd hoped for, but he got one, and he'd been able to fix things. He knew better now.

And he had a date at seven.

Yesterday, after that phone call, Teague had been nearly useless. It was a good thing that Avenstone was still waiting for the sellers to get their new counsel up to speed, since he would probably have been incapable of keeping his head in the game at lunch. He'd been worried he wouldn't be able to sleep, but all the late nights and high emotion at work must have gotten to him, because he'd slept like the dead. His head had hit the pillow last night and the next thing he knew, his alarm was going off.

He'd hit the gym and made it to work feeling better than he had in a week. Turned out to be a good thing—he'd gotten a call from Avenstone the minute he walked in, and they were off to the races.

He'd just finished up his third conference call for the day when there was a knock on his door to the beat of "Shave and a Haircut."

Carson.

Teague rapped his knuckles twice on his desk and in place of "Two bits" he said, "Come in."

Carson chuckled. "Good day?"

"Yes. Productive. Things are back on track, I think. A much better track."

"Excellent. Partnership, here comes Whitaker." Carson sat his very fine ass on Teague's desk. "How about dinner?"

"I can't, I've got plans." Very fine ass or not, he wouldn't have said yes, but it was nice to have a real excuse.

"Plans?" Carson looked incredulous. "Is your mom in town again or something?"

He snorted. "Nope."

"Sister?"

"Not this time."

Carson leaned closer. "Business thing?"

He sighed. "No, Carson. I'm meeting someone."

"*Meeting* someone? Wait. Like a date?"

"Yes, if you must know. It is a date." *And now maybe you'll back off.*

Carson snorted. "Right. Who the hell are you dating?"

Teague winced. Had Carson meant those words to sting the way they had? "Really? Do you have to be an asshole?"

"Come on, Teague. Where did you meet this guy?"

"Carson, if it turns into something you need to know about, you'll know about it."

Carson leaned back defensively. "Okay, man. I just kind of thought we had a thing starting here."

Whoa. What?

"Carson." They weren't starting a *thing*. They were never going to have a *thing*. Carson was smoking hot, sure, but a relationship? No. He'd thought Carson felt the same and was a little shocked to hear that his colleague wanted something more.

Teague was pretty convinced that he had a thing for someone else, in any case. He'd know for sure, shortly.

"I'm sorry, I just—"

"Nope. Don't. I got it." Carson stood up. "Your loss."

"I really am sorry," he lied.

Carson clearly didn't buy it and snorted at him before walking out of his office.

Great. Now he had office weirdness. He seriously didn't

need office weirdness. Maybe he could find a way to smooth things over with Carson later in the week.

It was time to head out. Teague had brought a change of clothes with him to work because he wanted Dallas to try to see past "Wall Street." He wanted Dallas to see *him*. He closed his office door and changed into khaki shorts and a plain white tee. It was too hot to get more dressed than that.

After his initial disappointment on the phone, he'd decided that meeting in person was a good idea. He ought to be nervous, and maybe he was a little anxious, but mostly he was just looking forward to getting to know this guy and confirming that what he'd felt the other night was real and not just fantasy and too much alcohol like the dancer had suggested.

He really wanted to know Jersey's real goddamn name.

It was a little bit of a hike to the West Village from Midtown, but he made it with time to spare. He found Johnny's and went inside, and after looking around the place, he settled on sitting at the bar where he'd be easily spotted. He ordered a soda. A plain, un-spiked ginger ale. He was thirsty and it went down fast while he watched the talking heads on CNN.

His date arrived spot on at seven. He felt a light hand on his back, and that was followed by a familiar voice. "Hey, Wall Street."

"Hey." Teague turned around and gave Jersey a smile. "Maybe we could go with Teague, please?"

"Oh." Dallas laughed. "Sure, Teague."

Dallas had on black-and-white striped shorts that pulled tight over his muscled thighs and a tank top that was more of a second skin than anything. His curly hair was mostly hidden by a backward baseball cap.

"It's nice to see you. Thanks for inviting me."

Dallas slipped onto the stool next to his. "This is crazy, right?"

Teague shrugged. "Maybe?" Probably. He started to say he'd done crazier things, but he didn't think he had.

Dallas glanced over at Teague's empty glass. "I was kind of hoping maybe we wouldn't drink tonight, you know? Just be—"

"Ginger ale." The bartender put down his refill and took away the empty.

"Oh." Dallas ducked his head and looked a little embarrassed. Teague couldn't help but grin at the way the man blushed. "Can I get a Diet Coke, please? Thanks."

"See, we're already on the same wavelength."

"Maybe."

"You're really unsure about this." Teague put it out there as a statement, it wasn't a question; Dallas's body language said it all.

"It's not personal."

"Yeah. It actually is."

Dallas's moss-green eyes watched him. "Okay. Maybe it is."

"It's weird, I guess. Awkward." He understood. They hadn't met under anything like conventional circumstance.

"I...don't trust this."

Oh, shit. Well, that wasn't good. He needed to give Jersey a reason to trust him. There had to be a million reasons to trust a horny total stranger, right?

Fuck.

"Diet Coke." The bartender set the drink down.

Dallas took a deep breath. "Can we get a table?"

"Oh. Yeah. Anywhere you want." Teague dropped some cash on the bar and picked up their drinks.

"Thanks." Dallas looked around a bit and chose a small

table way the hell away from the bar, off in a corner. "This okay?"

"Sure." Interesting choice, but fine.

Dallas sat with him. "Listen, before we start, I just want to say I'm sorry for losing my shit with you on the phone."

Teague put a hand up. "No. Stop. I was wrong to come by off-hours the way I did. It didn't even occur to me what handing an attorney's business card to your boss might look like. I hope you're not in too much hot water. And I heard you. I won't do that again."

Dallas smiled at him. "Cool. Thanks."

Teague let that smile wash over him and tried to keep eye contact. Dallas let him look for a minute and when the dancer blushed again, Teague realized that if he didn't leave here knowing Dallas's real name, his heart just might shatter into bits. He stayed as open as he could, hoping Dallas could see how earnest he was.

"What?"

Teague shrugged. "You asked me to come. I'm here."

"Yes. You have something to tell me?"

"You want to dive right into that?"

"Yes, Teague. That's what we're here for, right? I'm not a cowboy today."

"No. No, you're not. I get it." Straight to the point? Okay, then. Teague sipped his ginger ale and put it down again. "All right. I want to know if I bought that kiss or if you gave it to me."

Dallas's eyes widened. "That's not—"

"Not a fair question? Sure it is, Jersey."

"You're not supposed to be asking me—"

"Fine. I already know the answer anyway. I paid you, sure. But not for that kiss. That kind of kiss can't be had for money. It's not something that can be purchased. I know, because I can pretty much buy anything I want, and no amount of spoiling my dates has ever gotten me...*that*."

"Teague—"

Teague wasn't going to let him talk. Dallas had been clear and needed to listen right now. He held the dancer's eyes, gaze steady. "You want me to say what I said on the phone, but in person, right? Fine. Tell me that kiss was just a show. Tell me you didn't want more. Tell me you didn't find something you need in my eyes."

Teague stood up. "Tell me you don't see it right now."

"Where are you—"

He dragged his chair around to Dallas's side of the table and sat close.

"Uh. Teague."

Teague smiled, then leaned in quickly and kissed Dallas, cupping the dancer's jaw in one palm. Dallas made a brief attempt at a protest before the fingers that were pushing into his chest shifted and curled into the fabric of his T-shirt instead.

"Oh," Dallas whispered, softly, the sound barely more than a breath. Teague tightened his fingers over Dallas's nape and rested his other hand on the dancer's thigh.

By this point, with any other man, Teague would be mentally halfway to the other guy's apartment or hotel room. But not tonight. He was right here with Dallas, here in the bar, right at this moment. His chest was aching again, and it was the most important pain he'd ever been in.

Dallas reached up and touched his cheek, fingers on fire, burning their impression into his skin.

"I can't...tell you any of that." Dallas was a little flushed and breathless. God, he was lovely.

Teague nodded. He knew that. He knew it like he knew his own mind. "What's your name?"

"It's Jason," the dancer whispered, eyes heavy-lidded.

"Hi, Jason," Teague whispered back. He pulled farther away, sliding his chair to put a little air between them. "Thank you."

Jason smiled. "What the hell is happening?"

"I don't know. I feel like this is all backward, but I guess I wouldn't know. I haven't been...*here* before. Maybe it's always like this."

"Oh. Oh no, Teague. It isn't always like this."

Teague laughed. "Says a heart that's been broken?"

"Only a hundred times." Jason winked and picked up his soda. "You're the heartbreaker type, aren't you?"

"Maybe." Yes. A couple of times. Maybe that very afternoon with Carson, even. "It's not something I'm proud of."

"Not the best thing to admit to when you're trying to start something new." Jason laughed, though, softening the blow.

"Jason. The other night...I felt like my heart was being torn out of my chest."

"That ache."

"Yeah." Yes. The ache. A hollow, empty space that made him breathe deeper to try to fill it, and it only got more intense when Jason looked at him like that. A look wasn't enough.

Jason smiled. "I've been there."

"Been there."

Jason nodded at him, lifting his chin, leaning in just a little.

"Jason, I—"

Jason closed the distance between them in a rush, kissing Teague and cutting off his words. Teague returned the kiss, the connection making that deep ache a little easier to bear.

Or maybe just easier to understand. A kiss wasn't enough, but it made it better.

Teague reached out again and laid his hand on Jason's shoulder, running it down one pumped-up bicep. Good God, he hadn't ever dated beefcake before. All that muscle rolled and twitched with every move. Jason was like a mustang, small but powerful, muscles like an idling engine, stored up energy just waiting to burn.

And then it was gone.

Jason pulled away. "I've really enjoyed this." He stood up.

Teague leaned back in his chair, blinking. "You've... wait." *What?*

"This is where I would normally give you my number in case you wanted to call me some time, but you already have it."

"Wait." Teague stood as well. "Wait, you're leaving already?"

"This wasn't a date, Teague."

"It wasn't a—" What the hell was going on? "Jason, don't go yet." *I have so much to talk to you about. So much I want to know. I still don't know you.* But he wanted to. God, he wanted to.

"Call me."

"I don't understand."

"Good night, Teague. It was nice to meet you."

"...you too." *What?* He watched as Jason left the bar, sauntering right out through the door. Should he follow? Stop Jason? Let the dancer go? He stood there for a second, frozen with indecision, then took off at a run, bursting out onto the street and looking in both directions. He finally spotted the not-cowboy, halfway down the block and on the other side of the street.

"Hey!" Teague stepped off the curb and looked for his opportunity to cross, making his way up the one-way street in the wrong direction. "Jason!"

Jason either didn't hear him or was playing games with him because the dancer kept on walking.

"Hey!" Teague took off across the street, dodging cars, shouting like a loon and generally making a complete fool of himself. He didn't care. There was no way he was letting this night end like that. No way.

His feet hit the sidewalk and he burst into a determined sprint. He caught the dancer by the elbow and pulled him into a breathless kiss, ignoring Jason's yelp of surprise. He held on tight until Jason relented, moaned softly, and wrapped an arm around his neck.

"Teague," Jason whispered, panting against his lips.

"I couldn't. I couldn't let you go yet." He held on tight, one arm around Jason's waist and the other in the dancer's hair. "I'm sorry."

"You don't have to—"

"It's insane. I know. It's not rational." The words flowed from him, sounding desperate.

Jason searched his eyes. "Don't apologize."

"I just thought...I had different expectations. But it's okay. We can do it your way. I just—"

"Wanted another kiss?" Jason interrupted, grinning at him.

"*Needed* another kiss."

Jason nodded. "It was a nice kiss."

"It was." Jason hadn't tried to leave his arms, so Teague figured that it must be okay.

"You have to let me go now, though."

"Oh. I do?" He winked at Jason, who laughed at him.

"You do, honey."

"Man. That sucks." He let Jason slip away.

"Good night, Wall Street. Call me."

"All right, Jersey cowboy."

"Kiss my grits, sugar." Jason flipped him off and headed down into the subway, and Teague was left laughing alone on the sidewalk.

9

A t one o'clock in the afternoon, Jason was still in his pajamas. He hadn't made it home until after three, so he'd slept in. Ricky and Danny were still in their pajamas too. Well, Ricky had on sweats, and Danny had on a huge T-shirt that was obviously Ricky's.

"Good morning." Danny smiled at him, looking sweet and happy. He had to admit he felt a little jealous. Teague had texted him to say hello but because their schedules weren't matching up so well, he hadn't gotten that phone call yet—the one he really wanted, asking him out on a date. Teague had made apologies, new deal at work, crazy hours, and had said several times that the weekend was good for him. The weekend wasn't so great for Jason, though.

"Good morning." He handed Danny the box of Pop-Tarts he'd brought from the kitchen.

"Oh, sweet. Breakfast." Ricky reached into the box and pulled out a sleeve.

"Strawberry frosted, Jason? Wow."

"Is there any other kind?" It was his favorite.

Danny laughed. Jason noted smugly that his friend scoffed but took one anyway.

"I didn't get you guys coffee, but it's made." He had some for himself, though, a nice tall cup with a ton of cream.

He wanted to be curled up with someone right now. With Teague, maybe. Preferably. He just knew they'd work that way; he'd liked the way Teague held him. He loved looking into Teague's beautiful blue eyes. He could almost feel Teague's kiss still on his lips.

His phone buzzed, and he picked it up off the coffee table. "Oh. Yay!" It was Teague.

Working tonight?

Yes It was Saturday. He made his best money on Saturday nights.

Brunch tomorrow then?

That was a date invitation, right? *Brunch?*

Yes. Teague replied quickly. *Brunch. Coffee? Mimosas? Pancakes?*

Ooh. *I like pancakes*

I like you

Oh, flirting. Jason felt all tingly.

I like you too

So have brunch with me. Please?

"Should I say yes?" Jason asked out loud.

"What, honey?" Danny was just coming in from the kitchen with two mugs of coffee, and he handed one to Ricky.

"To a date. Should I say yes?"

"A what?" Danny sat and looked at him. "Someone asked you on a date?"

"Come back here, baby." Ricky, who was still lounging in the cushions, pulled on Danny's arm.

"Look." Jason handed Danny his phone. "That means a date, right?"

Danny read the conversation. "Brunch? Who is this guy?" Danny spoke out loud, texting Teague on Jason's phone. "This is Danny. I am Jason's best friend. Who is this?"

Jason made a grab for it. "Hey!"

Teague's response was to text a cute picture. Wall Street had on an Imagine Dragons T-shirt, his short, dark hair was damp, maybe from a shower, and his smile was toothy and adorable.

"Oh! He's so handsome. He looks like a total geek."

"He's a lawyer."

"He's a—" Danny looked at him. "Wait. Is this the same lawyer that came to see you at work the other day?"

He sighed. Danny knew? "You heard about that?" Did everyone know?

"Everybody heard about that. The rumors are fascinating. You're wanted on drug charges, you're in witness protection, you're actually a cop..."

"Oh, God. Really?"

Ricky sat up this time. "You're not a cop, are you?"

Danny stuck Ricky in the ribs. Hard. "Really. Romance is the least interesting theory, baby. But it's the one I like the best for you. Of course you should go on a date, Jase!"

"He's a guest. At the bar."

Danny blinked. "Oh. Oh Lord, Jase."

"I gave him a couple of lap dances and...and a kiss." The admission just popped out of his mouth, bypassing his filter. Not that he had a filter.

Danny put a hand on his knee and gave him a sad look. "It's a fantasy, baby. You know that, right? He's not into you; he wants Dallas." Danny looked back at Jason's phone, thumbs moving as he read out loud, "You need to back off. He's not a real cowboy. Keep it in your pants, asshole."

"No! No, no, don't!" Jason snatched his phone away from Danny and looked at the screen. "You didn't send that did you?"

Danny and Ricky started laughing. "I didn't even type it, baby. I just wanted to see how into him you were."

Shit. His heart was pounding. "You suck."

"I'd say he's into the guy." Ricky teased.

"Listen, as long as you're ready to get your heart broken by a guy in a suit that thinks wanting the hot, broke little stripper is romantic for five minutes, go have brunch. Fuck him if you want to. Why not? Just remember who you are and who he is."

"Jesus, Danny." Well, that was a downer. "What if he's not like that?"

"Do you know how often I've heard that?" Danny leaned back on the couch with Ricky.

Jason frowned. They were a good couple—Danny and Ricky. They looked good together, they had the same background, they were both no bullshit kind of people, they had a lot in common.

They were both broke.

They had the same schedule.

Fuck. Danny had a point.

But what if Jason wanted to believe that fairy tales could come true? What was so wrong with that? Maybe Teague did see past the cowboy. Jason wanted to find out what was behind that kiss—he knew there was more.

It was just brunch, right? He texted Teague.

How can I say no to that face?

Thank you! What's a good time?

God, not too early, he didn't want circles under his eyes. *11?*

Where?

Oh. Teague probably didn't live in Brooklyn.

"He wants to know where."

Danny was on that. "Midtown. Cute but not too pricey. Uh..."

"Blue Dog Café?" Ricky offered helpfully.

Danny nodded. "Oh, good idea."

"I've never been there." But what the hell. *Blue Dog?*

Midtown? I know it.

"He knows it." *See you at 11, Wall Street*

Okay, Jersey. Is it okay if I text you later?

Jason smiled. That was sweet. *Yes.*

Can I come to the club tonight?

It's a free country Wait. Wait, no. *Don't though, okay? Let's wait for tomorrow*

Okay, Jersey. If that's what you want.

That's what I want He wanted Teague to see Jason next, not Dallas.

Teague sent another selfie, this one of him giving a thumbs up. Jason took about seventeen selfies before he found one he liked well enough to send back.

"We're on for tomorrow."

"Okay, Jase. Tell me all about him."

He looked at Danny, knowing this wasn't going to go over well. "I don't know much."

"So, you just took a thousand pictures of yourself to find one to send to a near total stranger that you're trying to impress."

"I'm not trying to impress him," he lied. Of course he was. He had to make a good impression with his looks, right? He sure couldn't keep up with the cash.

"Then why not just send him the first pic?"

"Shut up." Jason sighed. "We have chemistry."

"You know that from a lap dance?" Ricky shook his head.

"No. I know that from the kiss."

"Oh." Danny grinned. "Okay, now we're getting somewhere. You want to fuck him."

"No! Well, yes. But that's not all. There's this...pull."

Ricky laughed. "I know that pull."

Jason rolled his eyes. "Would you guys quit teasing?"

Danny sat up again. "I just don't want you to get your heart broken, baby. That's all. Go have your fun. But you have to know what's up going in."

Teague had gone out of the way to get his name and had only asked for his first name at that. Wall Street wasn't pushing, wasn't rushing him. Teague had accepted that he wanted to date, wanted to do things the right way. In fact, he thought maybe Teague liked the idea too.

He sighed. "I get it, Danny. Thank you."

It was a little weird, he knew.

He couldn't expect Danny to understand when he didn't understand it himself.

10

It didn't take Teague long to decide that a Sunday brunch date was impossible to dress for. Brunch was supposed to be casual and laid-back. Sipping a warm cup of coffee, lingering over your food, taking it slow. Most guys he knew didn't even shave for Sunday brunch. But a Sunday brunch *date*?

Shaving was mandatory—that was a given. It was warm outside, but Teague went for blue jeans anyway, then had to think about his shirt. His mother taught him that a comfy T-shirt wasn't respectful on a date, and he'd sweat in a button-down, so he settled on a striped polo. Now that he was here, though, waiting outside the restaurant, he was starting to worry that it was maybe a little too collegiate frat boy for Jason.

Then again, what the hell, he could only be who he was. And he definitely had been a collegiate frat boy. Even now he was basically a frat boy, only he'd traded the sweats and baseball hats for a JD, an array of ties, and a handful of business suits.

He was supposed to be here, though. He'd known it as

soon as he got out of bed this morning, feeling the way he had the day of his first interview for law school. It was the same feeling as when he'd interviewed for his current job at the firm, and the night before he'd taken the bar exam. Every risk in his life that had been worth taking felt just like this, and the mix of anxiety and confidence was a strange but welcome cocktail.

"Wall Street."

He grinned and looked up at the name to find Jason a few steps away. "I work in Midtown, Jersey."

"I live in Brooklyn." Jason smiled, and it warmed him in a way the New York City humidity never could. "It's good to see you."

"You too. Thank you for coming." He lingered there awkwardly for a moment, not sure how to navigate the greeting. Jason finally offered him a hand and he took it, then leaned in and kissed Jason on the cheek.

"Mm. Are you ready for some coffee?"

He nodded and reached for the door, opening it for Jason. "So ready. After you."

They went inside and Jason gave his name. Teague barely heard it. "Kov...?"

"Kovacs." Jason nodded. "Mom says it's Hungarian."

"You're Hungarian? That's cool."

"No, I'm American. I don't know anything about Hungary, but I guess my dad was second gen."

"Is he gone?"

"From the house, yes. Since I was fourteen. From the world?" Jason shrugged. "I wouldn't know."

Damn. "Sorry."

"Don't be, please. Mom was enough, and I'm a grown-up now. That's ancient history."

They were seated, and getting his hands on a menu

made the moment feel a little less awkward, but that was one more thing that made them different. He'd basically had the fairy-tale upbringing.

"Mimosa?" He asked cheerfully as they got settled.

Jason smiled. "I'd love one."

Teague waved over a server and ordered two. "I'm actually pretty hungry."

"Well, let's make sure you eat, then."

"What's your favorite brunch food?"

"Mimosas? Coffee?"

Teague laughed. "Food. Are you a late breakfast or early lunch person?"

"Oh, late breakfast all the way. Waffles, I think. And bacon." Jason disappeared behind the tall menu, which wasn't that surprising since the dancer wasn't a very tall man.

"I like breakfast too, but I'm more the egg and sausage type."

"That is exactly what I would have expected, you know that? I bet you like fancy eggs too...Benedict or quiche."

"I'm looking at the *Croque Madame*, in fact." This version was open-faced and topped with fried egg. It sounded so good.

"Seriously?" Jason gaped at him, and they both started to laugh.

"Okay. I get the feeling you're making fun of me."

"I wouldn't." Jason made an exaggerated gesture like he'd been wounded, then laughed and sighed. "That's a lie. I totally would."

"I'm ordering it anyway," he shot back playfully.

"Fine, but you have to have a bite of my waffles, so I know you're really human."

"I can do that. And you have to try a bite of mine too."

Jason wrinkled his nose. "If I must."

"It's a deal, then."

"Mimosas, gentlemen." The server sat two lovely, tall champagne flutes in front of them, garnished with strawberries.

"Oh! So pretty." Jason's eyes lit up, their green shining in the light from a nearby window.

"Beautiful. And the mimosas look great too."

"Smooth talker." Jason picked up the glass, raised it to him, and took a sip.

"Just honest."

Jason gave him a sly smile. "Are you always honest?"

"Am I always honest? No. But I always tell the truth." Like that. That was truthful.

"Oh, that sounds shady, Mr. Lawyer."

"I know. But how do I answer that question? Are you always honest?"

Jason looked thoughtful. "No, I guess not."

"See? There's a difference between honesty and truth. If everyone was honest all the time, we'd piss each other off a lot more." He picked up his mimosa and took a sip, blinking at the bright, tart taste as the drink sloshed over his tongue. "Yummy."

"You're right. I hate to think the things that would come out of my mouth if I was always honest. I already have a filter issue." Jason laughed, the happy energy making Teague smile too.

"Uh-huh. And boundary issues too. You kissed me for the first time in front of an entire club. In a spotlight."

"Oh, Wall Street, you know you loved it."

"I did. But that kiss wasn't honest or truthful." Hot, but not honest.

"No." Jason grinned at him. "No, it wasn't either one. Not that one."

"But the next one..." He eyed Jason and took another sip.

"The lap dance? Yeah."

"You're not supposed to kiss a client like that, I'm sure." There were rules, and he knew that was breaking them.

"No." Jason blushed but didn't look away.

"That one was honest and truthful. That's the kiss that got me in trouble with you."

"Oh, baby." Jason touched his hand with cool fingers. "It's not that you were in trouble. I just—"

"I understand. I get it." Jason needed the work and was doing something he loved. "I didn't think that through. I won't fuck with your livelihood again."

Jason smiled and nodded, then took another sip of his mimosa. Sipping a mimosa wasn't supposed to be sexy, was it? But the way Jason did it, holding the tall, fragile glass by the stem just so and tipping the glass to his lips, it made Teague wish he were the rim of that glass.

He licked his lips, thinking about the honest and truthful kiss he was able to get on the sidewalk the other day. The day he'd known he wanted Jason at any cost. The day he'd agreed to take things slowly.

He was a total fool, but he was a happy fool.

"So...what's Dallas?"

"What's...wait. What?" Jason blinked at him.

He hadn't meant to make things heavy, but after the question came out, he realized it went deeper than he'd intended. "Well, Dallas is a character, right? A persona. Is he a truth or a lie? Is he honest?"

"That's work. It's not...it doesn't count."

"Everything counts."

Jason sighed, but he was thinking about it. "Well? I

mean, I love what I do, and Dallas is who I am when I'm doing it, so Dallas is honest, I think. Truthful, maybe not. But I'm still real, I guess. You tell me."

He nodded. "That sounds about right. No character is truthful, right? Anyone can wear a cowboy hat; that doesn't make them a cowboy."

"No, it just makes them look like a cowboy. Which, in my case, is a lie. But no one is getting hurt; everyone is just having a good time."

"So honest but not truthful."

"This is the most confusing conversation ever." Jason laughed. "Tell me about your work. You'd had a bad day the day we met."

"God. Had I ever. I showed up that night wanting to drink alone, look at something attractive, and forget the fact that I'd lost a huge—*huge*—client, and with it my job."

Jason sat forward, setting the mimosa down on the table. "Oh, my God. You lost your job?"

"No." He shook his head. "No, as it turned out, some wild miracle happened, and the client wanted to stay on and asked to work with me, specifically."

"That's crazy."

"It was crazy. That's just what it was. Impossible. But it happened."

"No wonder you were in a better mood the next day. Who was the hottie you were with that time? A coworker?"

"Yeah. Carson. He's a—" Teague was about to say that Carson was a nice guy, and maybe Carson was, but that road was dangerous too. "He has a thing for me."

"Ohhhh." Jason tilted his head. "Should I be jealous?"

"God, no. No. No way."

His vehement denial hit a nerve with Jason, who started laughing like a hyena.

"Shut up."

"Aw, you're stringing along a work-crush."

"I'm not stringing him along. I have made it clear I'm dating someone else. I was never the one with a crush by the way. Not on Carson anyway."

"That sounds awkward."

He nodded. It was. It was awkward that he'd let himself get involved with Carson at all. "Yeah. You have no idea."

"He was hot, though. Did you sleep with him?"

He nodded. "A couple of times. But I was...it wasn't planned, we were kind of desperate and definitely not sober."

"So, he thought because you'd slept with him that..." Jason trailed off, the implications clear.

"You know, I'm not sure what he thought. It's entirely possible that I misread him, and I was the total asshole. We work together—it never occurred to me he'd want more." He still needed to clear the air with Carson. He just couldn't leave it the way they had forever.

Jason shrugged. "Yep. Awkward. You couldn't find someone else to celebrate with that night? You must have a lot of friends in the city—ones that don't have a thing for you."

"Not...really." That was embarrassing but true.

"Oh, come on."

"No, it's true. I have friends in Boston and LA, one that's living in Toronto now. You know, college and law-school people. A couple of my classmates from law school do work in the city, but we're at different firms and we rarely see each other." One of them was married, and both were as busy as he was. He got the occasional text, but so far their schedules hadn't worked out.

"Rarely? Don't you need friends?"

"Well, I guess if I had time. I work a lot. My first year with this firm, I kept a sleeping bag in a cabinet in my office and slept under my desk sometimes. It was crazy. Very competitive. Those first couple of years as an associate burn out a lot of very smart people."

Jason gave him a look of horror and shivered. "Oh, my God. That's not worth it."

He smiled, understanding. "It's not for everyone, but to be honest, I kind of loved it. I'm glad I don't have to do that now, but I lived for it then." He'd made himself indispensable. He was the guy you could get on the phone at three a.m. He was the name people remembered, and he enjoyed that.

"That's good. It's good to find a job you love." Jason smiled back. "We have that in common."

"We do. And I don't sleep at the office anymore; that was just the early days. I do work a lot, though. I don't like to say no, and I don't like to be unavailable."

Their food arrived and Jason's eyes went wide. "Oh, my God, this looks amazing. Even your weird eggs look good."

Teague laughed. "Gee, thanks."

"Tell me about this guy you have a crush on." Jason winked and popped a bite of waffle into his mouth. "Mmm. Yummy."

Teague played along, cutting into his eggs, pretending to be casual. "Well, I met him at this bar..."

"Always risky." Jason took another bite of his breakfast and chased it down with coffee.

"It can be, but not this time. He's friendly and thoughtful, he loves his job, and he's smoking hot."

"Smoking, huh?"

"And he kisses like it's the most important thing he's ever done." That wasn't a joke. Jason's kiss was in some kind of league by itself. He'd always treated a kiss as foreplay, it was a stepping stone on the way to getting someone in bed. He'd never *just kissed* someone. Kissing and stroking off was about as innocent as it had ever been. But Jason's kisses made him want to stay in the moment, taste and touch, linger.

He glanced up from his eggs and into Jason's eyes and smiled. "His name is Jason."

A bewildered look crossed Jason's face along with a shy smile. "You made that guy up."

He reached across the table and took Jason's hand. "I didn't. That's both honest and truthful."

Jason tangled their fingers. "You're the good kisser."

He laughed softly. "I guess we'll have to find out later."

"Like a taste-test." Jason winked. "I'm so in."

"Me too." He wanted a kiss right now, so he kissed Jason's hand and let it go. "How are your waffles?"

"So good." Jason cut a bite and offered it to him. He took it carefully with his teeth and chewed it thoughtfully.

"Crunchy, sweet, and is that...what is that taste?"

"I think it's almond."

He nodded. "Delicious. Here." He scooped up a bite of his eggs. "Just try it. Pretend it doesn't have a big fancy name."

Jason looked at him skeptically. "Okay, but I'm not promising I'll—"

He forced the issue, leaning in with the fork so close Jason didn't have much choice but to open up. Jason took the bite and raised an eyebrow almost immediately, looking surprised.

"Uh-huh. See?" He leaned back in his chair and watched Jason, feeling smug. "Not bad, right?"

"Mm. Good actually. Wow."

"Don't sound so shocked."

"Well, it's just, I mean...who knew?"

"Uh...me?" He laughed. "How can you go wrong with ham and cheese and eggs and toast?"

Jason rolled his eyes. "I won't tease you ever again."

"Oh, please don't say that." Teague would let Jason interpret that however he liked.

———

"THAT'S A NICE PLACE." Jason took Teague's hand, squinting some as they stepped out into bright daylight. "Thank you for treating."

"You're very welcome."

By the time they left the restaurant, they'd killed two mimosas each and more than two hours. They'd even shared a cute little gelato thing for dessert. Jason hadn't had a meal like that in...well, he couldn't remember. Maybe never. He'd always been too broke to splurge on things and too busy to just hang out and relax. Money-wise, he was doing better now that he had work though—regular work, pretty good-paying work too. Maybe next time he could treat.

Next time. After Simon, and after promising himself he'd be single for a while, he couldn't believe he was thinking about a next time. His connection with Teague was impossible to deny, though. It was practically impossible to ignore too, and he'd tried. He'd tried not to get too excited about this date, to keep Teague at arm's length for—

"You okay?"

"Huh?" *Oh. Wow.*

"You went quiet on me."

Busted. He wasn't sure what to say. "Sorry. I was...thinking."

Teague took his hand. "Ah. Here's where the not always honest bit comes in, right? That's okay. I understand. I've been thinking a lot too."

"I was thinking about you." That was almost totally honest, right?

Teague hesitated so briefly that he was surprised he'd caught it. "That's..."

"Honest."

"Yes, it was." Teague stopped them, right in the middle of the sidewalk, and blue eyes searched his.

God, this was uncomfortable. You didn't stop right in the middle of everything like this, not in busy Midtown. People were having to walk around them and were making exasperated noises, but Teague didn't seem to notice. "We should maybe—"

"Mhm." Teague cupped his chin and kissed him, and Times Square went away as he lost his train of thought.

"Do you want to—" It was like they were in a bubble. His whisper was totally loud enough despite the bustling noise on the sidewalk.

"I'm Uptown."

"Of course you are." *Damn.* He was dating an Uptown boy. *Him.*

Teague laughed. "I'll try not to be insulted."

"Oh! No, no. I didn't mean it like that." God. He was so stupid sometimes.

"No? What other way is there?" But Teague had an arm around him and was leading him toward the subway, so how mad could he truly be?

He sighed. "Well, I don't know. I guess...maybe that was rude, huh?"

"No. It was probably accurate. I guess I come off privileged."

"Because you are." He'd never had a friend that was as financially comfortable as Teague, let alone a lover.

"Yeah. I know. But that doesn't automatically make me an asshole."

"Whoa, when did I say that? Way to get defensive."

"I'm not." Teague snorted and grinned. "Wow. Okay, maybe I am a little."

He kissed Teague on the cheek, trying to keep things cool. "Hey, is this our first fight?" First date, first fight, getting everything over with in one day.

Teague ushered him through the turnstiles, laughing. "I'm just teasing you, Jersey. But I'm all for kissing and making up." A hot hand gave his ass a squeeze and disappeared again as they stopped for an approaching train.

"Good timing." Danny was going to give him an earful, but he wanted Teague. He'd wanted Teague's hands on him ever since the night they'd kissed during that crazy lap dance. He couldn't even pretend that wasn't hot.

They didn't say much on the ride uptown. Teague held on to the overhead bar, and he held on to Teague as the subway train rattled along. He could feel Teague's tight abs against him and when he closed his eyes for a second, he breathed in his musky cologne. It was fine that they weren't talking, strangely romantic and not weird at all. They got off the train at 86th Street and walked a couple of blocks north and west to get to Teague's building.

"Wow." Jason looked around, feeling like he was on Mars or something. "It's so quiet up here. And bright. And... expensive looking."

Teague nodded. "It's quiet. I like it that way."

"Yeah?" He was a Downtown kind of guy. He liked people and the little bodegas, shops and dry cleaners... things that made the city what it was. "I think I'd get bored."

Teague led him into a building with a shallow but fancy foyer, lined with lots of shiny marble with polished chrome accents and huge mirrors on the side walls. It looked like a mini version of an upscale hotel, but no crowds of people and only one security guard sitting at a small desk.

"Afternoon, Mr. Whitaker."

"Hello, Chrissy. This is Jason," Teague said as they walked past her.

Chrissy gave him a nod.

And a once-over.

And wrote something down.

What the hell? He'd even dressed conservatively. Sort of. "She thinks I'm a prostitute."

"What?" Teague turned sharply to look at him. "No, she doesn't."

"She does. You didn't give her my last name."

Teague stared at him, then walked back over to the desk. "I'm sorry, Chrissy. Did I give you my boyfriend's last name? It's Kovacs. It's Hungarian. Jason's father was second generation."

Boyfriend? Oh, shit.

Chrissy looked at him. "Kov...?"

Jason sighed. "K-o-v-a-c-s."

"Thank you, Mr. Kovacs. Have a nice afternoon."

"Better?" Teague gave him a smug smile and stepped onto the elevator as the doors opened.

"You said I was your boyfriend."

"I wanted to make it clear she was wrong about you. Just in case you were right about her, which I still don't think you were."

"I was." He knew that look. "But...boyfriend?"

"At some point, Jason, you'll open your eyes and realize that I'm much deeper into this than you think I am. Possibly more than I should be, but these things don't tend to happen rationally."

These things? "But this is our first date."

"Second. Our first date was at Johnny's."

He shook his head. "That wasn't a date."

"I know you said it wasn't for you, but it was for me. I dressed for a date, I looked forward to it like a date. It was a date. A date that you ended early." Teague crossed his arms, watching him.

"Because it wasn't a date."

Teague laughed. "You just like to argue, don't you?"

"Only when I'm right." He gave Teague a coy smile.

"Ha!" Teague's eyes narrowed. "Denial seems completely in character for you."

The elevator doors opened, and they stepped into a wide hallway with only a handful of doors. One of them said "704" on it and Teague unlocked it.

"I'm not in denial. I never said that was a date. I said meet me." He'd needed to look into Teague's eyes, that was all.

Teague closed the door behind them. "I never said today was a date either, you know."

"Today is different." Obviously. This was a real date.

"Why?"

"Because."

"Because you say so, is that it?"

He laughed. He knew he was blushing, and he didn't care. "Yes. Exactly."

"So, I get to treat you like a date?" Teague moved in close, one arm snaking around his back and he gasped softly, the sudden move making his heart race.

He nodded dumbly. "Yes."

"I should probably warn you, I tend to want to make the first move with a date."

He stared into Teague's bright eyes. "I believe I have already consented to that, Counselor."

Teague's laugh was knowing, and his words were whispered against Jason's lips. "I believe you have." Teague's "first move" was a heavy kiss, the kind you only give someone in private, away from eyes, when you're getting ready to undress someone. He opened for Teague's tongue and met it with his own, hopeful that the little tangle they made was a promise of things to come.

Jason hummed and pressed closer, resting his hands on Teague's chest. Teague's nipples went hard under his fingers and he teased them through the soft shirt, thumbs working them in circles.

"Yes," Teague breathed into him and he nodded, tugging Teague's shirt loose so he could reach underneath it. Teague arched into him as he found the nubs again and he loved how sensitive they were, and the way it made Teague's kiss hungrier. Teague tugged at his shirt too and a breath later both shirts fell to the floor.

Jason leaned into Teague, who took one step, and another, with a curious grin on his face. "Where are we go —*oh*." As soon as Teague's back hit the wall, Jason bent and sucked a nipple in between his lips. Teague's fingers dove into his hair. "I like that."

"Mhm." He could tell. He sucked and nibbled gently, then switched and flicked at the other little nub with the tip of his tongue.

"I mean I really like that. You could—"

"More?"

"Yeah."

Jesus, that was a beautiful thing. He'd been there two

minutes and already found a hot spot. He sucked the little bud in hard and pinched the skin with his teeth, making Teague hiss and go up on tip-toe.

"Oh, fuck."

Teague's groan made his skin flush and his balls ache. He let go and licked the skin to soothe it but before he could move to the other side, Teague tugged on his hair and pulled him up into another kiss.

Then they were moving.

Their arms tangled as they tugged and wrestled with each other's jeans, slowing their progress toward the bedroom but not stopping it. They kicked off their shoes and socks and finally tugged their jeans off outside the bedroom door. Teague lifted him right off his feet and set him onto the bed.

"You okay? You good?" Teague asked, moving over him.

"So good." He was good. He was all in. But he could tell by the concern in Teague's voice that if he'd said he wasn't, Teague would have respected that. This was something Teague wanted, not expected.

A good guy. He'd wondered if that actually existed for him. He was more interested in the bad-boy side right now, though. He pulled Teague down and rolled up to meet him, both of them grunting as their hips met, finding hot, sweet friction as they moved together.

Teague was hard as nails, and Jason felt the slippery streaks Teague's cock left as it slid against his hip. Their kiss was so desperate, their teeth clashed together between bouts of chasing each other's tongues.

"I've been thinking about this since the night I met you."

"You mean the night you met Dallas?" Jason teased.

"No. You. I saw more than Dallas. You didn't believe it, I know, but I did. I do. Your eyes are bad liars."

They were rocking in rhythm now, their breaths coming and going at the same time. "You don't know me yet."

"Not everything. But I will." Teague reached between them and palmed his dick, rolling the head under a hot hand before the curious fingers moved to grip him.

"Teague—"

"I'm a fast learner," Teague purred at him. Jason nodded and arched into the touch, his body begging for more. "Look at you. So lovely."

"Oh. So sweet." So sweet it made his heart ache. He gasped and let his legs fall open, giving Teague more room, feeling like he was on fire.

"You want me?" Teague whispered.

"Yes."

"Are you sure?"

He thought at first this was a game, but the look on Teague's face wasn't playing. "I am. I do. God."

That muscled frame stretching long as Teague reached past him to find protection in the nightstand. That little bit of potential first time together awkwardness just...wasn't. At all. Jason enjoyed every second watching Teague's face as the thing went on: the way Teague bit his lip concentrating, the hot little grimace, the satisfied sigh. Teague could even make a fucking rubber hot.

"Want you, baby. Come on." Jason hiked his knees up, knowing just how shameless he looked.

Teague was totally into it, licking his lips and pouring some lube onto his fingers. "Such a hurry."

Teague touched his hole and for a horrific second he thought he might pop right off like a teenager, but he didn't. His ass rippled, though, fluttered like a butterfly's wings, welcoming Teague's intrusion. "God."

"That works. 'Baby' or 'lover' will also do."

"Shut up and touch me."

Teague rumbled his approval and moved slowly, teasing him for a bit with one finger, then adding a second, making Jason moan and hike his knees up higher. "So hot, Jason."

"Need you." Jason looked down his body and watched Teague stroking himself slowly with the other hand, prick heavy and hard.

Those blue eyes locked on him. "Is that good?"

He nodded and a needy moan escaped him. "Yes. Yes, more—"

"You want more already?" Damn that teasing tone. He hadn't wanted anything this much in ages.

"Yes. Fuck, yes. Teague." *More, a lot more. All of it. Now.* "Please."

Teague nodded, eyes narrowing, and reached for one of Jason's knees, bending it farther back as that thick cock breached him slowly. He gasped, sure he was going to shatter to pieces, but Teague was steady and took his time, so kind and careful he thought he might cry instead. Teague let out a shaky exhale as their bodies came together and Jason tucked his hands around Teague's ass, squeezing and pulling them even closer.

"Yeah. Jesus, Jason." Oh, Mr. Tease wasn't so together now, was he?

"Fuck me, baby," Jason taunted, talking Teague up. "God, you feel so good."

Teague tensed for a second and let go, taking him in strong, deep strokes, finding a powerful rhythm. Jason struggled to move, to meet Teague's thrusts, though there wasn't much he could do in this position but welcome the burn, let it happen and enjoy it.

He could tease, though.

"More, baby. Give me more."

That earned him a groan. "Damn, Jersey."

Mmm. Somebody liked that. Jason took a breath and went on. "Come on, baby. Give me more of that beautiful, fat cock."

"Fuck." He got a nod and Teague found another gear, hips working hard, breath going ragged.

Hell, yes.

"That's it." He hauled on Teague's ass and leaned up to take a kiss.

As their lips met, Teague surged into him, claiming his mouth. Long fingers tangled into his hair, holding him down. He tucked his knees in against Teague's hips for leverage and bucked, loving how it made Teague cry out even as it set off fireworks behind his eyelids.

"Teague! Fuck!"

"Want...oh, God. Jase."

"Close, baby. S—*oh, fuck*. Again there...right..." Teague touched him just right, inside and out, and fire burst in his belly as his balls emptied, pumping over and over, spraying Teague's ribs.

"Oh, shit. Tight, Jase..." Teague lost his rhythm, and after a wild round of fast, shallow strokes his big, blue eyes glossed over, and Teague's mouth dropped open in a silent shout.

Jason gasped; the way Teague's cock danced inside him made him shiver, and his breath came in short, shallow pants. Teague was making amazing sounds—moans and soft grunts, the involuntary noises of a man who'd been out of his head and was slowly returning to the room. Sexy sounds.

Satisfied sounds.

He lowered his feet to the mattress and pushed his fingers into Teague's hair. "So good, baby."

Teague nodded and seemed at a loss for words still. Instead of words, Teague kissed him, the gesture slow and gentle, lazy. The words Teague finally found were, "Beautiful."

Oh.

Teague's words—or, word—struck him, and Jason replayed it in his mind, holding on to that moment. He could've cried. He didn't, but he honestly could have. No one ever told him he was beautiful, and for once it didn't matter whether he believed it; he believed Teague did.

Their eyes met and it shocked him how open Teague was, how relaxed, blue eyes holding his easily. He smiled, trying to meet Teague in that space, feeling free...and safe.

They settled together, still catching their breaths, his head in the crook of Teague's shoulder and Teague's arm firmly around his back. He didn't know how to say what he was feeling, but he made sure to touch, moving his fingers across Teague's smooth chest. Teague hummed happily for him, breath slowly transitioning to a deep, even rhythm.

Jason sighed as he too, drifted off.

11

Sundays were made for lazy, and they didn't get much lazier than this. Teague lay there as the room grew dim and dimmer still, curious what time it was but not really caring. He had his arms around his new lover and was in no hurry to move. He and Jason were spooning rather aggressively; he had one arm over Jason's chest, holding him in, and Jason pressed into him so they were very close: chest to back, hips to ass, knees curled together. He nestled his nose into Jason's curly hair and the man smelled so good, like the beach in summer—but not the way suntan lotion smelled—more like a fresh ocean breeze with a hint of salt and sand. He couldn't imagine what it was, but he loved it.

Teague listened to his lover breathe and tried to reconcile how vulnerable Jason was allowing himself to be right now with the man who hadn't wanted to offer up his real name over the phone just days ago.

Given all those reservations and their non-date date, it seemed a little soon to be lying here like this, on Jason's part at least. But he'd asked, he'd made sure, and he had no doubt Jason wanted this as much as he did. Not one shred of doubt.

Damn.

I mean, damn. Pushy as hell too. Hot damn.

Hot being the operative word. Jason had been alight. On fire. And mouthy. He liked that a lot. Teague was convinced this was the beginning of a wild adventure, and he was looking forward to all of it.

Would it be tricky? Sure. They wouldn't be able to live in each other's back pockets with their disparate schedules, but that was okay. That was how these things went, and either they'd work, or they wouldn't. He sincerely hoped they could figure it out, and he certainly would make it a priority to try. He needed to be focused at work right now, anyway. His schedule could be erratic, though, and they might even get lucky and have some lazy late mornings once in a while.

Not as lazy as this lovely Sunday. He'd have to try to keep Sundays open.

"I hear you thinking." Jason didn't twitch, but the voice was clear enough.

Teague laughed. "That loud, hm?"

"You're the loudest thinker I have ever known."

"Is that so? I believe if you look at which of us has been overthinking this relationship, you'll find it isn't me." He kissed Jason's smooth, bare shoulder.

"This is a 'relationship,' now?"

"Thank you for making my case so succinctly."

"Suck what?" Jason's giggle vibrated against his chest.

He rolled his eyes. "Succinctly. Sorry. It means concise. Brief."

"Why didn't you just say brief?" Jason rolled onto his

back and hooked his legs over Teague's knees. "And where is your sense of humor? That was funny."

He grinned. "I'm an attorney. Why use plain English when you can make things perplexing and convoluted?"

"Ha! I know what perplexing means, Counselor. Nice try." Jason stuck out his tongue, or tried to, despite his big grin.

Teague laughed. Jason was so real, and he loved that. No pretense, no smoke screens, Jason was pretty much himself all the time. Sure, he'd seen moments of discomfort or insecurity, but those were just as real, probably more so. "You have a spectacular ass." Jason blushed. "And you're the hottest thing ever when you come."

"Carson told me I look like I'm choking." He'd thought Carson was teasing, but it hadn't struck him as funny.

"He's a prick. I'm glad you're leading him on. Break his heart."

"I'm not leading—" *Oh. Damn it.* Teague grinned sheepishly.

Jason waggled his eyebrows. "So serious all the time."

"So mean to me."

"Never."

They both laughed until it devolved into sweet, slow kisses. Teague sighed, nuzzling Jason's cheek. "This has been a great day."

"Definitely in my top ten." Jason kissed him again, gently. "No, top five. Definitely."

Teague decided right then and there that making spot number one was a goal. "Are you hungry at all? You want to order something? Or I have some cheese and veggies and tortillas."

"Starved. Do you have guac?"

"I have avocados."

"Good enough." Jason sat up. "Let's cook. Can I wear one of your dress shirts?"

He blinked at Jason. "Can you, what?"

"I've always wanted to do that. Walk around in a lover's dress shirt. It's a thing. Can I?"

And to think, he usually couldn't wait to get out of them. "Sure. In the closet. Just pick one you like."

"Oh, yay. Thank you." Jason didn't take long, finding a professionally starched pink oxford and pulling it on. It was long, plenty long, but Jason did find his briefs and pulled those on too. "How do I look?"

Teague pulled on sweats and looked Jason up and down, smiling. "Adorable. Sexy. Like you're staying a while."

"I approve of all of those things." Jason winked at him and left the room. "Oh! Look how nice your living room is. My God, a grown-up lives here."

He hadn't given Jason a tour—they'd been so caught up in each other when they arrived. His living and dining room had a fireplace with artwork over it, a leather couch and an overstuffed chair, a square dining table at one end next to two tall windows with plush curtains. His desk in the corner was a disaster of paper and manila folders. His laptop was under there somewhere, he was pretty sure.

"It's comfortable."

"It's all color coordinated, you have art, and the furniture all goes together. You have four matching chairs at your table. I'm impressed." Jason walked through the room, trying out different places to sit and settling in the big chair. "Oh, I like this."

"You look good in it." Like a model. He wanted— "Can I take a picture?" He wanted a picture of Jason in that shirt, lounging in his chair.

"Oh. Is that...? Will you not share it?"

"Share...oh. I don't do social media." He didn't have any idea how those apps worked. His firm had media people for that. He still made actual phone calls with his cell phone.

"Okay, then sure." Jason grinned and bounced in the chair, trying out poses.

Teague laughed and grabbed his phone. And by that time, Jason had settled on sitting with his legs artfully draped over one overstuffed arm, ankles crossed, the dress shirt barely covering the important bits. Classic Playgirl pose. He approved. "Oh, I like that."

Jason smiled sweetly, evilly, and tried a smoldering look. He got all of them. "Perfect. You're hired." He put the phone down, but Jason hopped up and grabbed it.

"Let me see." Jason held the phone up to Teague's face and it unlocked.

Clever.

"Not bad. I look like I ate something sour in this one, though."

"No, you don't. And I'm keeping it anyway."

Jason handed the phone back. "Those better not end up blackmail."

"Really? Are you worried you'll lose your job as an exotic dancer over a sexy but tasteful photo of you in my chair?" Teague laughed.

"Maybe you have a point, but shut up."

They both started laughing again and he took Jason by the hand, pulling his lover into the kitchen.

"I'll make the guac. I'm picky as hell since Danny taught me. You'll be glad I did, I make it right."

"Are you implying I can't make good guacamole?" He pretended to be insulted, but he actually had no idea.

"Yes," Jason deadpanned.

"Snob," Teague teased.

"That's funny coming from a man who uses spelling-bee words in casual conversation." Jason found the avocados like a hound sniffed out a fox. "Jalapeño? Cilantro? Lime?"

"Would you believe I have all of those things?" He hadn't planned on making guacamole, though. He figured he'd better pay attention in case he wanted to make it for himself.

"And you have tomato and onion, of course."

"Of course." Thank God. How humiliating would that have been?

The next twenty minutes were a humbling lesson on everything he didn't know about chopping onions and tomatoes. He was so pathetic in Jason's estimation that Jason didn't permit him to cut up anything else.

"You can grate the cheese. For the quesadillas."

Oh, boy. How was this going to go over? "I buy it grated..."

"Oh. Okay." Jason glanced at Teague and looked back at the jalapeño he was dicing, doing a terrible job of hiding his disapproval, and he didn't say anything else.

Note to self, buy good cheese.

Had to keep his man happy. And cooking. This was fabulous.

Finally, Jason sat a bowl down in front of him with a bag of organic chips he'd bought at Whole Foods. Jason seemed to approve of those and dipped one into the guac, then handed it to him. "Try it."

Teague took the chip, and Jason crossed his arms over his chest.

He took a bite.

No lie, it was the best guacamole he'd ever had anywhere ever. And this was New York. He'd had plenty. "Oh, that's outstanding. Delicious." He reached for another chip.

Jason grinned happily and also helped himself. "Right? So good."

"Oven's hot for the quesadillas." He was proud he remembered.

"Oven?"

Uh-oh. "Well, you have to melt the cheese..."

"Oh, my God. You're in detention." Jason waved a hand at him. "Where are you from?"

"I do that wrong too?"

"Jesus. Yes. Get me a skillet." He loved that Jason had just made himself at home in his kitchen.

"I can do that." He had a stocked kitchen. A full complement of pots and pans, and gadgets his mother and his sister had given him as gifts that he almost never used. He was perfectly glad to have someone around that knew what was what in the kitchen.

Teague handed over the skillet, a spatula, some oil, the cheese...everything Jason asked him for. Jason was in his element and way too much fun to watch work.

He'd been permitted to chop the peppers and onions this time, but that was all. He did make margaritas, on the rocks with salt, and Jason approved of those.

They brought everything out to the dining table and sat there looking out over the street. "I like it here. I sit here when I need to just people-watch and let my mind wander. This is where I hang out when I have time to let myself enjoy a cup of coffee and unplug for five minutes. You know? It's nice."

"It's a good spot. The view is great. Do you get sun?"

"In the morning, yes." Teague decided to get bold. "Are you working tonight?"

"No. I have today off. I work tomorrow night."

"So stay and see it yourself. Have breakfast in the sunshine with me tomorrow morning."

Jason smiled, covering his blush with a bite of quesadilla. "Oh. Yum. We did good."

"Did we?" He picked up his fork and let the invitation rest. Pushing it wouldn't get him a "yes." He could tell Jason liked the idea but had reservations. He'd come back to it later and find out what they were. "Oh, we did."

The guacamole was outstanding. Teague made note of the recipe for himself but was secretly hoping to keep Jason around to make it for him. The quesadillas were much better done on the stove than in the oven too, better texture, more taste. He'd never been a great cook, but he enjoyed trying.

He'd made the margaritas a little strong. He hadn't done it on purpose, but when the table went quiet as they ate he knew he'd hit some kind of nerve by asking Jason to stay, and he was glad for the little bit of liquid courage.

"Okay. So...what did I say?"

"Hm?" Jason looked up from his plate, mouth full.

"I asked you to stay tonight, and you haven't said a word since."

"Oh, I'm just hungry. You know, can't talk, eating?" Jason tried out a smile, but it fell flat, uncertainty evident in his lover's eyes.

Hopefully he could use that term truthfully.

"It's not a big deal, Jason. If you're uncomfortable staying, just say so. I don't mean to rush you." He didn't want to put pressure on Jason. That said, he knew asking was bold, and he was lying anyway; it was a big deal to him. He wanted Jason to stay.

Jason carefully put his fork on his plate, reached for his hand, and tangled their fingers. That could have been a good thing, meaning that Jason wanted that connection, or it could have been a bad thing if Jason wanted to let him down easy.

Shit, is it good or bad?

"I want to stay, baby."

And here comes the "but." Goddamn it.

"I'll stay. But we have to talk about what happens next."

"What do you want to happen next?" He squeezed Jason's fingers. Okay. Jason was staying, that was good. "I'm in."

"I'm serious, Teague."

He grinned. "You must be. You just used my actual name."

Jason made a goofy face at him. "Damn it. I mean it. We need to talk."

He shrugged. "So, talk. I'm going to say yes to whatever you say."

Jason pulled his hand back and crossed his arms. "That's not a talk. That's just you telling me what I want to hear."

"What's wrong with hearing what you want to hear?" He just wanted Jason to be happy.

"Because that's not a talk, baby."

"Uh-huh. There you go trying to start a fight again," Teague teased.

"Would you—I am not!"

He laughed. "Are too."

Jason stood, reached across the table, and punched him in the arm.

"Ow!" He was still laughing.

"Shut up. You so deserved that."

He so did. "I did. I did, I was teasing you. I'm sorry. I'm glad you're staying." Teague took Jason's hand again, playing with Jason's fingers until they relaxed. "I want you to stay, you want to stay. This is good, right? Go ahead. I'm listening, I promise."

Jason watched him and the longer they looked at each other, the more that doubtful look on his lover's face faded. "Okay, fine."

Teague winked at Jason and went back to his breakfast without a word. Whatever Jason had to say, he was ready for it.

"Well, it's just our schedules."

He'd thought about that too. "Yeah. They're a little off, I know."

"A little? You work all day and I work all night."

"But neither of us works all day every day." Usually. He had a bad week now and then.

"How are we going to do this?"

Wow. Jason was really stressed about this. Teague put his fork down and caught his lover's eyes. "We're going to spend every minute we can together. What else can we do? We'll text. Send pictures. Talk a lot. It's not like this disappears when we're not in the same room anymore."

"Are you sure?"

He thought he understood what Jason was asking. He answered the question Jason had asked first. "I'm sure." But he wanted Jason to have the rest of his answer. "We're exclusive, right?"

Jason blinked at him; then those eyes lit up happily. "I just wanted to be sure."

"I thought so. We are. We'll figure it out."

"It'll be hard, though. You know? For you, and your job..."

Judging by the way Jason was watching him, he knew his new lover was looking for something specific. Sure, maybe Jason was fishing a little, but it wasn't such a bad thing to look for some reassurance, was it? He didn't think so. To Jason, this probably felt like a huge risk. Teague didn't completely understand it; he didn't think he'd done anything to make Jason feel insecure, but he looked Jason square in the eye anyway, smiled, and said, "You're worth the effort."

Jason exhaled with a soft laugh. "You keep saying all the right things."

"Are we going to argue about that too? If so, I'll need another margarita first."

"Oh, for Christ's sake." Jason's exasperated sigh got them both laughing.

"Look. This is still new, and we need to be respectful of that. Neither of us can really have expectations yet, right? If we want this to work, we're going to have to figure it out together. Put the thought and the time in. Find our rhythm."

"And we're monogamous."

Teague nodded. "I already promised that."

Jason's eyes were full of mischief. "Are you sure you can stay away from your coworker?"

God, he was so done with Carson. He was pretty sure he'd pissed Carson off enough to make it a nonissue now, anyway. "I'm sure. Can you manage not to pick a fight for five minutes?"

"You." Jason launched toward him, assaulting him with a hard but playful kiss.

He yelped, a strangled, startled sound that was muffled against Jason's lips. He gave in easily though; he'd take those kisses any way he could get them. Jason found a nipple and rolled it under one finger, just gently but fuck, they were always so sensitive. The touch sent a bolt of electricity to his balls, and a moan escaped him.

"You really do like that," Jason whispered, breathing into him.

"I do." Teague traced Jason's lower lip with his tongue.

"Well, damn." Jason climbed into his lap. "I know how to get your attention."

"You have it. You walk into a room and you have it." It was a little scary, actually.

"Take me back to bed, Teague."

"I was just going to offer you some wine."

"Offer me some wine in bed."

"I can do that." He hooked an arm around Jason and levered his lover right off his lap. Jason stood but stayed close, leaning on him as they made their way down the hall to the bedroom. "Climb in, beautiful."

"Oh." Jason blushed. "Really?"

"It's the truth." He nodded, heading to the kitchen for wine.

And honest, too.

12

Jason sat in a chair in the dressing room before his shift, feet resting on another chair, and soaked up the air conditioning while he scrolled through his text messages. The ones with Teague. Again.

Good morning, Gorgeous.

There were plenty of texts like that one from Teague: _Good morning. Good night. How was work? What are you up to today? I miss you._

Texts about the plans they'd made to see each other—plans they had actually kept. Three overnights last week and two this week so far. A handful of last-minute meals together. A stack of hours at Teague's, the apartment quiet while Teague worked and he read or watched a movie.

And a bunch of pictures. A picture of a dead rat in the subway station. A picture of the view from Teague's office window. A selfie of Teague with a crazy stack of paper on his desk, a Starbucks cup, and a goofball smile. That one was his favorite so far.

None of the pictures were rated X or even suggestive. Teague hadn't asked him to send any, either. In fact, none of

Teague's texts over the last two weeks had wanted anything more from him than to connect.

This was unreal.

He wondered if anyone would believe him if he said there was at least one hot gentleman left in the world.

Well, two. Chris Evans seemed like a straight-up guy also.

It had been two weeks since their first date. Well, okay, no. It was only Friday, so not quite. Twelve days, eight hours, twenty-seven minutes and—he looked at his watch—fifty-four seconds.

Fifty-five.

Fifty-six.

Fifty-seven...

But who's counting?

He laughed at himself and scrolled back up to the most recent text from Teague, the one he hadn't answered yet. Sometimes you had to let a man think you were busy, right? That you had a life.

"Hey, honey."

Jason looked over his shoulder. Danny hurried over to kiss his cheek and he turned his phone off and put it away. "Hey, what's up?"

"Just early to cool down before I go out there and sweat more."

"Right?"

"I don't know why you don't just stay with your man; he must have air conditioning."

Oh, that was good. Clever. "I was home because I worked late, and he had to get up early. I don't like to wake him up."

Danny smiled at him. "Oh, good. Ricky and I were worried you'd broken up."

"Broken up? Geez. We're barely even together yet."

"Uh-huh. And what was so secret that you had to hide your phone when I came over? Did he send you something dirty? Something hot? Can I see?"

"No! What? Stop that."

"I'm right, aren't I?" Danny snorted.

"No." But he still didn't want to show Danny the text.

"Bullshit."

"It's none of your business."

"None of my—" Danny gave him a haughty look and strutted away to another chair at another dressing station. "Fine. Some best friend you are."

"That's not fair. Maybe it's private."

"Maybe?"

"Private enough." Jason rolled his eyes.

"Is it a naked selfie?" Danny looked hopeful.

"No, but—"

"Is he professing undying devotion?"

He snorted. "No." But there was a little heart at the end of the text.

"Is he plotting a murder and asking you to bring a shovel?"

"Danny—"

"You just don't want to show me." Danny turned his back and started pulling clothing out of his bag.

"Oh, fine." He got up, pulled his phone out, and marched over to Danny to show him.

Danny read the texts and made a face. "*That's* what you didn't want me to see?"

"Yes. It's Teague's formal headshot from his law firm's website." Teague was in a blue suit, a white shirt, and a striped tie. The lighting made Teague's hair seem a lighter brown than it actually was, and all that color made his eyes even bluer. He looked handsome as hell.

"A little uptight, huh?"

Jason sighed. "See? This is why I didn't want to show it to you."

"He looks hot for a corporate jockey."

"He's not a—don't be an ass, Danny."

"I just can't believe you're dating someone like him." Danny closed his bag.

Someone like him? Danny didn't even know Teague. "Why? I'm not good enough for a lawyer?"

Danny sighed. "That's not what I mean, baby. He's just not...you're a club dancer. He's..."

"Stop. Stop now and don't say what you were about to say."

Aaron poked his head into the dressing room, interrupting them. "Look alive. Shift starts in twenty."

"Thanks, Aaron." Jason turned on his heel and went back to his own dressing station. Fuck Danny. He and Teague had something real. Was it perfect? No, but it was good. Was it forever? After two weeks he wouldn't know. No one would.

"Don't be like that, honey."

He started changing his clothes, slowly putting on Dallas, starting with his shorts. "Don't talk to me, Danny."

"Oh, come on. You know what I meant. I just worry."

Jason nodded. "I know exactly what you meant. Teague and I are working on something good."

"Ask to meet his fancy lawyer friends."

"What?"

Danny pinned him with a look. "If he's totally good with you and who you are, he'll be excited to introduce you right?"

"Of course." Teague wasn't embarrassed by him. They'd been out together a lot.

"Okay, good."

"Good." Jesus, that pissed him off, though. He eyed Danny as he finished dressing and stomped into his boots. "If you cared about me, you'd just be happy for me. What did you say to me earlier? Some best friend you are." He popped his cowboy hat onto his head.

He didn't need that shit. He had tips to make. A good man to keep happy. He pulled out his phone and read the rest of the text from Teague again.

I'll be there tonight to cheer Dallas on and take you home with me.

He liked that a lot. It was just the right level of possessiveness, a little show of dominance. Not "Do you want to come home with me?" No, it wasn't a question at all, was it? It made him feel wanted. Needed. It turned him on.

That was what he was going to focus on instead of Danny's idea that maybe Teague was slumming it by dating him. That he wasn't good enough for Teague and his corporate law firm and his business suit friends.

He'd given one of those law firm friends a lap dance, hadn't he? And fuck if the guy hadn't loved it. So there.

Jason tucked his phone back into his bag, shook it all off, and stepped out onto the floor as Dallas. He adjusted his hat and smiled, making his way into the crowd standing at the bar. He hadn't been out there five minutes when a hand pressed against his stomach.

"No touching." He brushed the hand away. This was how his night was starting off? It was eight o'clock, and the handsy nutjobs were out already, huh?

Jason wandered past a table of young men and stopped, leaning on it. The young guys loved him. "Hello, boys."

The cute blond in the middle looked him over. "You're a little far from home, aren't you cowboy?"

"Yessir. I'm Dallas."

That got a laugh from a couple of the guys; then the one with the dark beard chimed in. "I think I've fucked someone named after every big city in Texas. Austin, Dallas, Houston—"

"You lie. You did not fuck a Houston."

"I did."

"Bullshit."

"Boys," he tried to interrupt and steer the conversation back to, well, him.

"When did you—did you fuck an El Paso?"

"Shut up."

"How about a wacko from Waco?"

The bearded guy launched himself at the blond and the table they were at tipped over. Jason was about to move but was hauled out of the way by security before he'd taken two steps. The whole thing was cleared up in half a minute. *Boom.* Gone.

Well, that was fucked up.

"You okay, Dallas?"

Keith was a good guy. A big guy, too. He looked up—like, *up*—and smiled. "I'm fine. Thank you for looking out for me."

"You're welcome. You don't weigh anything. I don't want you getting hurt."

He crooked a finger at Keith, and when the big man had bent down far enough, he kissed Keith's cheek. "You're good to me. I better get back to work. Thanks again."

Keith blushed and shook his head, grinning. "Yeah. Get back to work."

He just laughed as the big man walked away, then did just that. He flirted with a couple on the dance floor. Then he chatted up a cutie that didn't have any cash on him. Just when he was about to head over to the bar a huge, heavy hand landed on his ass.

And squeezed.

Jesus Fucking Christ. Was there something in the water?

He stepped away and started to turn around to reprimand the guy, and a twenty flashed in front of his eyes. "Want a dance."

"Well, all right, sugar." He plucked the cash out of the guy's hand. "Is this a tip?"

"There's more."

"Well, come on, then." He wasn't sure about the size of this guy—mostly the big ones were softies—but just in case, he gave Keith a wave before heading back. He got a quick nod in return.

"Where are you from?" he asked, making conversation.

"Out of town."

"Out of town like Jersey, or out of town like Mars?"

The guy laughed. "Chicago. Here on business."

"Yeah? What kind of business?"

"None of yours."

Whoa. "It's just small talk, sugar."

He led the way into one of the private rooms, and the guy followed close behind him. Close enough that he was glad he'd alerted Keith. He glanced over at the two-way mirror, and the lights flashed.

All good.

"What was that?"

"DJ. You have a name, Chicago?"

"That will do."

Jason snorted. "What do you want to hear?"

"You. Moaning."

He blinked at the guy. "I meant music."

"None. I just want to hear you." Chicago ran his hand

along the edge of a clear and very present erection under his jeans.

It had to be a full moon, right? All the crazies were out.

He stared hard at Chicago. "You know the rules? No touching me at all. Clear?"

Chicago nodded slowly.

"Take your shirt off."

"Not part of the deal."

The guy pulled out a fifty and waved it at him. He looked at it for a long moment, then reached out and took it. He stuffed it into his pocket with the twenty he already had and unbuttoned his shirt.

"I'll give you another fifty to take your shorts off."

"Not gonna happen, sugar. Just enjoy the view you got."

"What's underneath them?"

"How about I put some music on?" He waved at the window and club music came on loud.

"Aw, come on." Chicago shouted as he started to dance, waving him closer.

Right. A lap dance needed a lap. *Shit.*

"No touching." He straddled Chicago's lap and started to move.

It was fine for a bit, the guy was touching himself but not Jason, and the music kept him distracted. He liked club music. The continuous *whomp-whomp-whomp* always made him feel a little high. He liked to dance too, so as long as Chicago kept behaving, he was having a fine time.

He turned around to give the guy the back view and that was when things started to go sideways. Those huge hands landed on his ass again—both this time—and when he turned to remind Chicago there was no touching, the guy yanked his shorts down.

After that everything was a blur. Heavy hands landed on his bare skin, and a second later he was moving—or being moved —the music cut off and there was shouting and chaos. Finally, the room went completely silent, and he was alone for a minute.

He looked himself over and pulled up his shorts. He was okay. He was totally okay.

God.

He bent over, scooped his shirt off the floor, and put it on.

You're okay.

He sighed and looked at himself in the two-way mirror to straighten himself up.

"Dallas?"

He practically jumped out of his skin when the door opened. But it was a familiar voice. *Aaron. It's just Aaron. Breathe. Jesus.*

"I'm okay."

"I'm glad. He's out. Banned. Okay?"

Oh, good. That was good. Jason took a deep breath and moved away from the mirror. "Okay. Thanks."

"You were smart to alert Keith."

"I just...I had a feeling."

"And you were right. You have good instincts. Next time just say no."

He blinked at Aaron. "I forgot I could say no."

"Any time. Private dances aren't required. I'm not gonna say I've never insisted and made it worth a dancer's while if it's one of my VIPs, but most of the time if you boys don't like the vibe, I'm gonna back you up. I'm all about my bottom line, but that one dance isn't going to matter, and you're zero good to me if they break you."

His entire opinion of Aaron changed at that moment.

Jason threw his arms around his boss and hugged him. "You're the best."

Aaron didn't quite return the hug, but he got a pat on the shoulders. "You've earned it. You work your ass off for me."

"Thank you."

"Let me go, kid." Aaron snorted.

Jason let go abruptly, feeling himself blush, cheeks going hot. "Sorry."

Aaron gave him a nod. "You're good?"

"I'm good."

"Good. Go have a shot of something on me and get to work." Aaron clapped his shoulder and left the room, leaving Jason bewildered and blinking.

Full moon. Had to be.

After a deep breath, he headed for the dressing room to clean up a little; then he ducked behind the bar and got that shot of you-got-this he'd been promised. He wanted to be over it all before his man showed up.

Teague walked in about nine, alone, and somehow even in a club full of every kind of man on earth, his man stood out. Jason had assumed Teague would go home and change, but instead his lover looked almost exactly like the night they'd met. Sharp suit, loose tie, handsome frown. *Damn.* It must have been a long day.

He wanted to go right over, but he was deep into tempting a group of hotties that wanted dances. He gave Teague a smile when their eyes met and Teague smiled back, so how bad could things be?

"Who are you smiling at, cowboy?"

"A Wall Street hottie," he teased, getting an idea. "I think he wants a dance. Are y'all in or what?"

That seemed to light a little fire under their indecisive asses and two of them spoke up, pulling out their wallets.

Score.

He smiled and took their cash, not at all worried about either one of them, and led them toward the private rooms. He marched them right past the bar like the Pied Piper and Teague turned around on his barstool to watch them go by.

"Dallas." Teague nodded.

He reached over and tugged on his lover's tie. "Hello, Wall Street."

"Busy night?" Teague looked tired, but he got a smile.

"I'll find some time for you, sugar. Sit tight." He winked at Teague. "Come on, boys."

He swore he could feel Teague's eyes on his ass as he walked away.

It was over an hour before he finally got a chance to visit with his man. "I'm so sorry, baby. I hope you didn't come expecting to spend a lot of time with me tonight. It's so busy."

"No. You're working, I know. I'm good. I'm people-watching."

"You should have brought someone to hang out with." *So I could meet them and make Danny eat his words.*

The words he hadn't let Danny actually say.

"Maybe next time. Tonight I just came to watch."

"Just watch?"

"Can I kiss you?"

Jason gave Teague a flirty grin. "No, but I can kiss you." He leaned close and planted a kiss on Teague, a Dallas-brand kiss, heavy, but no tongue.

"Mmm."

He felt Teague's moan, but it was too hard to hear over the music. He put a hand on Teague's chest and pushed gently, breaking off the kiss. "That's enough, Wall Street."

"No, it's not." Teague's eyes were smoldering.

"Well, it will have to do for now, won't it?" He was doing his best to stay in character, but Teague's presence was heavy and obvious and making that hard.

Teague's look was smoldering too. "I'm patient."

"Really? Are you?"

Teague laughed. "Okay, no. No, not at all."

"Uh-huh. You just came here to check up on me."

"Check up on—" Teague eyed him. "You're trying to start another argument, aren't you?"

"What? No." Much.

"I'm going to win this argument at my place later."

"We'll see about that."

"Ooh. I like how that sounds."

"Ladies and Gentlemen!" The spotlight spun around the room and finally landed square on him.

"Just for that..." He made a show of giving Teague a playful shove, hopped up onto the bar and moved a few feet away. He grabbed a cute little blond by the collar and gave the boy the kiss that always started his set. The "So there" head toss he gave Teague got a bunch of laughs from the men at the bar.

Teague's eyes rolled, and his lover gaped at him as he strolled right past and down the bar to where Keith was waiting to help him.

If there truly was an argument to be won, he'd was pretty sure he'd just dropped the mic.

This bit had become routine fun now—the trip to the stage, the little striptease, the dance. But it was different with Teague watching. He still enjoyed it, but this time he wasn't just dancing, he was dancing for his lover. It was weirdly hot. Teague was obviously enjoying it, and the crowd was too—he raked in quite a little pile of bills around his feet. But lost in his performance as he'd been, it wasn't until the song ended and he bent to grab all the bills on the floor that he realized he had a pretty decent boner going.

Well. Shit. That explained the cash, but how fucking humiliating. Fuck the full moon. He was glad for the stage lights because they helped him hide his blush in the shadows until he got off stage.

He made a beeline for the dressing room to put his cash away and hide for a second, but he should have known better. He got a sound teasing once he got there. It was all in good fun, though; he wasn't the first to have a boner onstage and he wouldn't be the last. But this was his first—how was he not going to worry every time?

Tell Teague he couldn't hang out at the club?

Maybe. Maybe that was the answer.

He stashed his cash and cleaned up *again* before making his way out to watch Danny's performance from the bar, as usual, even if he was mad. He didn't think Danny was right about Teague, but he also understood. He didn't have anything close to the money he assumed Teague had. Money was scary. It divided people. It kept people together when they shouldn't be and apart when they should be together. Danny was being his friend and looking out for him, even if he was wrong.

He sighed. He'd invite Danny for coffee tomorrow, and they'd talk it out. He couldn't stay mad for too long.

Danny's music was already playing and he hurried to the bar to watch, arriving just in time to see the crowd parting close to the stage. That was new; Danny must have changed it up. He'd been thinking maybe he should do the same, but that bar kiss thing was always a big hit.

Danny was lifted onto the stage, and a guy in a suit right behind him.

Teague.

His eyes narrowed and the hair stood up on the back of his neck.

You asshole, Danny.

He watched Danny slide Teague's jacket off, skin crawling. The two of them danced together a little, but mostly it was Danny moving and Teague watching and grinning. The cash piled up for Danny too, and as the song ended, Danny held one of Teague's hands up like a prize-winning boxer.

The crowd went nuts, and Danny topped the moment off by kissing Teague. Kissing his man, on stage, in front of a crowd. In front of him. And what the fuck was Teague doing up there, anyway? Teague kept it short, though, pulling away as the crowd cheered, scooping up his jacket and heading off the stage as Danny gave a wave and gathered up cash.

He turned around, hands on the bar, mind going a hundred miles an hour. Teague appeared next to him before he'd had a chance to figure out what he was feeling or what he wanted to say.

"Hey, cowboy. That was a hoot, huh? I can't believe that dancer talked me into that."

"Danny."

"That's it. Danny." Teague leaned in for a kiss and he turned his head away. "Oh. You're working, right. Sorry. I've had a couple."

"You already got your kiss from Danny."

"Yeah. I didn't know he was going to do that. That was a little over-the-top, huh?"

He flicked his eyes up to Teague's face. His lover was flushed, a little sweaty and a little tipsy, but those pretty eyes were focused on him. He smiled despite himself. "You looked like you were having fun."

"I was. That was crazy. Wait. You're not mad, are you?" Teague put a hand on his arm. "Are you mad? I swear it was just...are you mad?"

He sighed. Teague had no idea what Danny was up to, so he couldn't be that mad about it. It wasn't fair. "No. No I'm not mad at you, baby."

"Oh, good. We were just talking, and that song started playing, and he dragged me over. I guess I'm just—I didn't think about it. I'm sorry. I won't do that again."

"What were you talking about?"

"Oh, nothing. Bullshit. He was asking me about work and about our *second* date."

"First." He let himself grin. "First date."

"You're a pain in the ass."

They both laughed, and he leaned in for that kiss he'd missed out on a second ago. Teague had it for him, and it was warm and right, it was a kiss just for him. Teague would never have kissed Danny this way.

He wanted to believe Teague had never kissed anyone this way.

"Pretty," Danny interrupted. "But you better get back to work, honey, before Aaron has kittens."

They ended the kiss, but they didn't just break it off, they let each other go gently. Jason turned his head and raised an eyebrow, letting some of his anger show. "Nice try, *honey*."

Danny crossed his arms over his chest. "Really?" The challenge didn't help matters.

"You're an asshole, Danny. What the fuck is wrong with you?"

"I'm sorry, I was doing my job and investigating the corporate slug."

"The...excuse me?" Teague leaned forward.

"And as it turns out, I like him. He doesn't seem like the

dick I was worried he was at all. He might actually be into you."

"Well, gosh, thanks for that." Teague stared at Danny.

Jason snorted. "You had to take him up in front of a crowd to figure that out?"

"No, that was gratuitous fun. But he didn't try to steal my spotlight or my money, so he won some brownie points." Danny's grin wasn't the least bit apologetic.

He touched Teague's hand. "I didn't send him to spy on you, baby. I swear."

"Okay." Teague tucked an arm around him. "Well, I didn't tell him anything I would be ashamed for him to pass on to you, so I guess we're in the clear on this one."

Danny stared at Teague. "Listen. What kind of friend would I be if I didn't check you out for myself? It's my job."

"Oh..." Teague pointed at Danny but looked at Jason. "Best friend?"

Jason and Danny both nodded. "Best friend."

"Got it." Teague nodded slowly. "Can I buy you a shot of something, Best Friend?"

"If you're still here at the end of the night, Wall Street, you know it." Danny's grin was wide and happy. "Are you still mad at me, honey?"

Jason shrugged. How mad could he be? He might have been insulted, but Danny was looking out for him. Danny had been working at the club for a long time and had seen a lot in this place. "I wish you'd have just trusted me."

"I will next time." Danny smiled.

"Next time?" Teague looked horrified and made them all laugh.

"Really, Jase. I'm sorry." Danny opened his arms for a hug, and Jason nodded and gave him one.

"What? I don't get an apology?" Teague was probably

expecting one of them, but a hug from them both at once definitely surprised him. "Whoa. Thanks."

"All right, lovebirds. Everybody back to work." Aaron's tone was friendly, but Jason knew his boss meant business.

"Baby, if you're bored sitting here, go home. I'll come over after work."

"Nope. I came to see you dance," Teague protested.

"And you saw me. I don't dance again for an hour."

"Then I get to watch you work." Teague leaned against the bar.

Jason rolled his eyes. "You're impossible." He gave Teague another peck on the cheek. "I'll see you around, Wall Street."

"I work in Midtown." Teague winked at him, those baby blues full of affection, and Jason suddenly understood what it meant for your heart to skip a beat.

He knew this was big, what was going on between them. It had a four-letter name, but he didn't even dare think it. It was something he'd been painfully wrong about recently and had decided he wasn't looking for right now.

It was a cowboy's prerogative to change his mind, right?

———

THE NEXT TIME Teague came to see him at the club, he was going to insist his lover go home at a more reasonable hour. By the time his shift was over, Teague looked so tired, and no wonder. The man was probably at work at some crazy early hour that morning, like, *nine*, or something. *Ugh.* Jason didn't understand how anyone got up that early.

"This is an obscene hour to get off work, you know."

"It's only a little after two, Wall Street. I've left as late as four."

"Four a.m.? Jesus. I don't think I've seen that hour since my days as a first-year associate."

"Depends on the money I'm making and whether my lover is waiting for me." He wasn't leaving early exactly, but there was certainly still a little money to be made. He'd done well tonight, though; he wasn't hurting by going home.

Teague glanced at him. "Sorry. Am I eating into your bottom line?"

Jason laughed. "Oh, Teague. So many things I could say right now."

"Ha!"

Keith opened the door for them. "Home safe, Dallas."

"Thanks for the assist tonight." Jason reached for Keith and slipped some cash into the big man's pocket.

"You're welcome. And that's appreciated. See you tomorrow night?"

"You know it."

The door closed behind them, and Teague took Jason's hand.

"What was that about? Oh. I think that's our—"

"Hey. Cowboy."

"Fuck." Chicago, the handsy big guy from earlier tonight stepped right into their path. Jason froze for a second and squeezed Teague's hand. "Get lost, asshole. You've been banned."

"They can't ban me from the sidewalk." The guy took a step closer.

"You heard him. Step aside, please."

Step aside? Oh, Wall Street, that wasn't going to cut it. He was pretty sure that was their car at the curb, though. They just needed to get in and get out of here. He'd explain to Teague later.

Jason tugged on Teague's hand and started to head for

the car, but the guy reached out and poked Teague in the shoulder.

"What's the plan, sport? You taking the hot cowboy home?"

"Get out of our way."

Jason squeezed Teague's hand again and let go. Keith. He'd just bang on the door. "Don't, Teague. I'm going to get—"

Just as he stepped away, Chicago gave Teague a hard shove.

"Hey! Hands off, asshole." Jason was torn between running for the door and running to Teague, and as he stood there frozen and indecisive, something fucking amazing happened.

Teague not only kept his balance, but his lover hauled back and launched a fist at Chicago that connected solidly and, by the look and the sound of it, broke the guy's nose.

"Damn, Wall Street!" Jason hopped into action, banging hard on the club's side door. Keith answered, and all Jason had to do was point, and it was all over.

Keith ran for the guy while he was still disoriented and blinded and Chicago hit the sidewalk.

"You got this, man?" Teague asked, rubbing his knuckles.

"You got a good hook, brother. I got this. Take Dallas home."

Jason moved quickly to Teague's side, moving him toward their ride before they lost it.

"You want me to stay for the cops?" Teague was watching Keith, but he let Jason move him toward the car.

"I've got that covered."

"Come on, baby. Keith is a pro. You don't want to be here when the cops come."

"I'm not that worried about—"

"Get in the car, dummy." Jason smiled and opened the door.

Teague sighed and got in, and he climbed in right behind. He took Teague's hand as they drove away. "You hit him hard."

"Yeah well, I knew I had to. With someone that big, I wasn't getting a second shot. Thanks for grabbing Keith."

"It was awesome. Hot. I feel all proud of you."

"Thanks, Mom." Teague laughed gently. "Oh. Hurts right there."

He ran a thumb over the sore spot gently. "I think it's just going to be a bad bruise. I have arnica and ibuprofen at my place."

"I think I have Advil—"

"And weed," Jason added.

That got him a nod. "Your place sounds great."

Jason looked up at him, and they both started to laugh. Teague asked the driver to head to Brooklyn instead of Uptown, which was kind of a no-no in the Uber world, but they worked it out.

"Jesus, that guy was huge. What was that about anyway?"

"He got handsy earlier. Keith rescued me and Aaron banned him." And that was all pretty cool, actually. That people were looking out for him.

Teague looked at him hard. "Rescued you?"

"I'm fine, baby. I promise."

"What would have happened if I hadn't been there?" Teague sounded worried so he played it down.

"You were. It doesn't matter."

"Well, it does. What if he comes back?"

"Relax. He's from Chicago, here on business. He won't."

That didn't seem to make Teague feel much better. "So he says. Keith was looking out for you, huh?"

"He was. And Aaron said I had good instincts. I'm fine, you know. Shit happens. They took care of it. I did like eight or ten more lap dances tonight, and they were all fine. Let it go."

Teague raised an eyebrow at him. "Are you telling me not to worry, or to mind my own business?"

"Are you really that worried?"

Teague shrugged. "I am. I want you safe."

"I mean, it is my job. It's not like I'm not going to work tomorrow. It's not like things are going to change. You and I both know it could happen again, right? You can't worry all the time."

Teague didn't look happy about that answer, but he didn't get grumpy either. "I know. It just hadn't...I hadn't thought about your work that way until now. That's all."

He understood why Teague worried about him. It meant his lover cared. Teague had been great about everything else —his dancing, other guys looking at him, throwing money at him, the lap dances and all the flirting. All of that, and Teague hadn't said a word or seemed jealous or anything. Teague was just looking after him.

I want you safe.

That was sweet of Teague to say. The only person who'd ever worried about him was his mom. Well, and Danny.

And Teague was the first man ever to throw a punch for him.

Huh. So this is what people did when they gave a shit? The least he could do was give a shit back.

"I'll talk to Aaron and make sure there's security close by when I take guys back, okay?" He wasn't sure it was possible to have someone like Keith there all night, but there was always someone in the booth keeping an eye on the cameras. It wasn't like he'd ever be totally alone.

"Thank you. That would make me feel better."

He kissed Teague's bruised hand. "I'm sorry about your hand. Thank you so much for doing this for me."

Teague nodded, put an arm around his shoulders, and kissed his temple. "You're very welcome. It's just bruised, it'll be okay. Hopefully Keith will scare that guy off for good."

Jason had no doubt. "He will. Keith is good like that."

13

————

Teague kept Jason close, snuggling his lover all the way to Brooklyn. He kept his arm protectively around Jason, feeling himself relax a little at a time as Jason breathed beside him.

It occurred to him as the car pulled up outside Jason's building that this was an opportunity to prove Danny wrong about him, prove that he truly cared and wasn't just fucking Jason because the man was pretty. Jason was hot as hell, that was a fact, but he wanted his lover to have more faith in him than Danny did.

They headed inside to find one of Jason's roommates awake, plus Danny, who was leaning against him on the couch; already ahead of them with a graceful and tall glass bong in front of them on the table.

"Hey! You brought Wall Street home with you." Danny smiled from his spot tucked under the crook of the man's arm.

"I did. Have a seat, baby, let me get you some ice." Jason ducked through a doorway, which he assumed led to the kitchen, and he smiled, determined to do this right.

"Hello again, Danny." He waved at the other guy with the hand that didn't have the bruised knuckles. "Hi, I'm Teague."

"Ricky. Hit?" Ricky nodded to him and offered the bong. He smiled and took it easily, finding himself a chair.

"Thank you."

"Jason! He might be a keeper!" Danny shouted.

Teague laughed as he shrugged out of his suit jacket. "Might be?" He wanted to be a keeper.

When Jason came back into the room with beer and a bag of ice, Teague was already lighting a hit for himself with Ricky's bong. He caught Ricky giving Jason a thumbs-up out of the corner of his eye. So far so good.

He didn't feel like he needed anyone's approval, but it was good to know he had it. Especially from Danny. Best friends could be influential.

"Smooth, right? Ricky has connections." Jason took the bong from him as he leaned forward to put it down, but Teague touched a finger to it and Jason lowered it to the table.

"I don't get a turn?" Jason's curious pout was adorable.

He winked and crooked a finger at his lover, holding his breath.

"Ooh. Shotgun?"

Teague nodded again.

"Oh hell, yeah." Jason grinned and moved closer. "Awesome."

He tugged on his lover until Jason was straddling his knees. Jason accepted the kiss and Teague exhaled, gently forcing the potent smoke right into his lover's lungs. Jason's fingers curled into his shirt and held on.

How fucking hot was this?

"Damn, Teague. I think I totally misread you."

He wasn't perfect, but he appreciated Danny's comment all the same.

Teague watched as Jason held the hit in as long as he could manage, eyes dilating noticeably, until he exhaled slowly, releasing a trail of smoke into the room. They finished it off with another kiss, deep and slow, making him moan. God, so fucking sexy.

Keep this up and we're not gonna be social for long, lover.

He wasn't ready to leave the room yet, though. He knew how things looked: that he was privileged, and Jason wasn't, that it would be easy to read his intentions all wrong. He was genuinely into Jason. It was important to him that his lover's closest friends accept him; there was no way this would ever work otherwise.

Jason rested the ice on his hand and snuggled into the crook of his arm. "I need a shower."

The ice was shockingly cold, but the mellow high was just starting to kick in, and he liked it. It had been a while since he'd had a smoke. "You want company?"

"It's a small shower."

"So, what does that mean, we have to be close?"

Danny shook his head. "We tried it, Teague. Ricky and I don't fit. We made it work, but I had the knobs in my back and Ricky—"

"I hit my head on the shower nozzle. Not awesome." Ricky laughed.

Jason pulled away from him. "I'll just be a quick minute, baby."

He kept their fingers tangled until they couldn't reach any longer and his hand fell back into his lap with a plop. "Damn. I like showers."

Jason giggled and disappeared, closing a door behind him.

"That's his room." Ricky offered helpfully, eyelids heavy and speaking slowly. "That one is mine over there. Shamus and Lee share the big one at the end of the hall. And we have a part-time roommate, Poe. He travels for a living, but when he's in town he takes the couch."

"You have a lot of roommates."

"Got rent to pay, and none of us makes great money. Well, none except Jason now, who seems to be kicking ass."

"He's good." Danny nodded. "I knew he would be. He wasn't so great at keeping jobs before. He'd stay two weeks or a month and quit. He hated everything. But this job he says he likes, so..."

"Maybe he should have been an actor. He loves performing," Teague offered.

Ricky snorted. "Don't tell him that; he's making better money where he is. Actors are even worse off than I am."

"What do you do, Ricky?"

"I'm a dancer." Ricky looked proud for a second and sighed. "Well, I'm supposed to be. Right now I'm tending bar. It's good money."

"That's a great side-hustle. People are always looking for good bartenders. It's a tough job."

"It can be. But it pays the bills and then some. Lee is trying to finish college, Shamus waits tables at La Jolie."

"Oh, that's a nice place. I had lunch with clients there last week."

"I'll tell him you liked it." Ricky snorted and shook his head. "Maybe he waited on you. I hope you tip."

Danny laughed. "You're actually eating lunch at the high-priced restaurant where Shamus works. That's...wow."

He looked between them, then leveled Danny with a serious look. "All that means is that you know I can take care of Jason if he needs me."

Danny watched him for a long, silent moment and nodded. "I know. But his last man had a little money too, and that turned out badly, so you're just going to have to deal with me looking out for him. Sorry, not sorry."

He raised an eyebrow. "I get it. You don't trust me yet, and you care about him. He's lucky to have you."

"What'd you do to your hand?" Ricky asked, pointing at the ice with his chin.

"Oh. Well...I hit a guy that was bothering Jason."

Danny's eyes went wide. "At the club?"

"After. Jason said the guy had gotten handsy and was thrown out. He came out of nowhere when we were leaving and started hassling Jason on the sidewalk."

"We have bouncers..." Danny suggested.

"Yeah, well. Jason ran to find one and I...stopped the guy from following." He pulled the ice off his knuckles and stretched out his fingers. He was fine, didn't need the ice at all. "It was hell on my manicure," he joked, just for Danny's sake, goofing around with an exaggerated and snooty accent. "I'm going to have to get my chauffeur to take me to the salon tomorrow before all of my minions see me."

Danny rolled his eyes. "Okay. All right. Cute, Wall Street. I get you. Funny, funny."

Ricky grinned and filled the bowl again, then held out the bong. "You want another hit, man?"

"Sure. Thank you."

"You're all right by me. I never liked that French fry Jason was seeing before anyway. He kept dressing Jason up and showing him off like a prize pony."

He shrugged. "I just want to be with him."

"Right on."

"What does your traveling roommate do?" He lit the bowl and took a nice hit, wincing at the burn at the back of this throat.

"Poe? Oh, he's a roadie. He's on tour with P!nk right now."

"He's badass. He's built like a refrigerator and he's covered in ink. He wears these huge boots all the time."

"Always has this big-ass smile on his face, though, nice guy. Quiet. Pays the whole month when he comes to stay even if he's only here for a week. He and Lee used to be a thing, but they're just friends now."

"With benefits?"

"Sometimes, yeah." Ricky laughed. "If Shamus is into it, he'll share."

That was all the breath he had, so he exhaled as slowly as he could manage so he wouldn't cough. "Oh, I feel good. Thanks for that."

Ricky held his hands out, making a "help yourself" gesture. "Hey. Enjoy."

Danny climbed into Ricky's lap, and Teague took that as his cue. He stood carefully, because he was feeling a little comfortably numb. "I'm going to head to Jason's room. Good night."

"Night, Wall Street."

He chuckled. "I work in *Midtown*..." Not that it mattered anymore. The name had stuck, whether it was accurate or not.

He ducked into Jason's room and had a look around, surprised by the sparseness of it. The bed was neatly made with a simple black comforter on it. There was a tall dresser and a matching bedside table—just one—that were in good shape but not remarkable, and probably from Ikea. One tall lamp on the other side of the bed, and a window with a box fan in it. He went and stood in front of it for the air. Jason's room was warm.

The walls were mostly bare, though there was one poster of a band he didn't recognize, and a calendar hanging next to the dresser.

Very simple, almost no personality. So odd for a man who had so much light inside.

Teague heard the water running still, so he rapped on the bathroom door and went in. "Hey, it's me." He let the damp, warm air sink into his skin. It didn't feel that much worse than the bedroom, honestly.

"Hey. I'll be out in a second."

"No rush, just checking in on you."

Jason stuck his head out around the shower curtain. "I've been showering alone for a long time, baby. I'm fine."

He laughed. "I'm stoned and lonely."

"Oh...Ricky got you hooked huh? You'll be his next customer."

"Does he deal?"

"Oh. Yeah. Shh. Don't tell anyone." Jason disappeared into the shower again.

"Who would I tell?" It was weed. Who even cared?

The water shut off and he was hit with a wave of damp air as Jason opened the shower curtain. "Hand me that green towel?"

"I got it." Instead of handing it off, he tucked his hands into it and started drying Jason off, starting with his hair, working down to his shoulders and abs.

Jason watched him. "You're drying me off."

"I am."

"It's weird."

God, he loved that smile. "Bad weird?"

"No...not bad. It's kind of sexy."

"Mhm." He drew the towel over Jason's chest and around to his back, working the thick terry against Jason's skin and over all of Jason's tight muscles. He lowered his hands to that perfect ass and got a double handful, then started on each leg.

"I kind of feel spoiled." Jason rested a hand on his shoulder.

"Good. I'd like to spoil you." He caught Jason's cock and balls in the towel and tried to dry them clinically, but he failed pretty badly. Mostly on purpose.

"Mm." Jason hummed at him. "What else would you like to do to me, Counselor?"

He took his time with his answer. He turned Jason toward the mirror and swiped a swath of fog away with the towel before hanging it up. He finger-combed Jason's curls, catching his lover's gaze in the mirror. "I would like to get my hands on every single inch of your skin, work my fingers into your tired muscles, and make you melt right into your bed."

"You...really?" Jason bit his lip.

He nodded slowly. "Really. Do you have oil or lotion?"

"You're serious? I ache everywhere after that crazy night."

"I know, I could see it in how you were walking. Like your back was sore, your legs?"

Jason nodded. "You don't have to—"

"Where's the oil?"

"On my dresser."

He took Jason's hand and led him to the bedroom.

"Come on. Let's get in front of that fan where it's cooler and let me get to work."

While Jason found the oil, he pulled his shirt off and hung it on the closet doorknob. Then he kicked off his shoes and slid out of his dress pants, folded them, and sat them on the dresser. "I hadn't planned to be at your place—I'm going to be doing the walk of shame in a wrinkled suit tomorrow."

"And won't everyone be jealous? That sounds just perfect."

He smiled. "Making lemonade with lemons?" He tossed his socks down with his shoes, feeling much cooler in just his boxers.

"That's my favorite thing to do, baby. I've been handed a lot of lemons. I'm good at it."

"Maybe I'll just keep you in bed all day, and I won't have to walk home at all." That sounded wonderful, but he knew what Jason's answer would be.

Jason sighed. "I have to work at—"

"Seven, I know. But until then, I can keep you in bed. Stretch out, Jersey. I'll make sure you're feeling good for later."

Jason stretched out, and Teague had to admire all the muscle for a minute. Every time Jason moved, something rippled or twitched; it was fascinating to watch, and beautiful. He put a little of the oil in his palm to warm it and spread it over his fingers before starting in on his lover's shoulders. Big muscles first to help Jason relax.

"Oh..." Jason's groan was just right, validating that what he was doing felt good. He'd worked in a massage with lovers as foreplay, but it wasn't about that this time. He let it be sensual, because he enjoyed the touch and he couldn't hide that, but it wasn't a means to an end. Whatever it led to, including sleep, was fine with him.

"That's it, just relax. Concentrate on my touch, the heat on your skin. This is a lovely oil, is it...sandalwood?"

"Mmhmm. It has arnica in it and something else. Healing things, I was told."

"So you've used it before?"

"Ricky rubbed my back and my feet after work the first couple of weeks. I was adjusting, it wasn't...like this. We're just friends. This is better."

"Well, I'm sure Ricky has great hands, but he probably doesn't enjoy touching you as much as I do."

"Mmm. Baby, you say the best things." Jason sighed and he could feel his lover's shoulders relaxing, the tension easing.

Teague thought being a little high for this was nice. He wasn't in a hurry, and he totally lost any sense of time as he happily immersed himself in the feel of his lover's skin.

The room fell silent after that except for Jason's soft groans until Teague hit a knot in Jason's calf. "Ooh, that's... ow. Right there."

"I got you. Just breathe." Teague worked that knot loose and a handful of others, then moved on to the smaller muscles. He worked on Jason's hands, making his lover chuckle weakly. He was careful with Jason's feet because he didn't know if Jason was ticklish, but he needn't have worried—Jason fell fast asleep before he finished.

He did the other foot anyway—a whole-body massage wasn't complete until it was a whole body; then he very gently moved off the bed and went to clean up. When he got back, Jason had curled up on one side and was out cold, which he thought was the best compliment he could get. He'd taken care of his lover, made him feel good.

Teague climbed into bed with Jason and spooned up behind him. Every day felt like an adventure right now.

There was so much he knew and so much he didn't. One thing he did know; those two guys in the men's room that night who he'd envied so much didn't hold a candle to this. This was the realest thing he'd ever had. It didn't matter that it felt like a dream.

14

Aaron caught Jason as he arrived at work. "Hey, Dallas, you okay?"

"Huh?" Oh. Right. Last night. Teague had massaged the memory and all the stress that went with it right out of him. "Yeah. I'm good, just tired." He'd crashed hard for a while, but when he woke up in the middle of the night, feeling fantastic, he'd made sure to say thank you.

After that, Teague just hadn't been able to keep his hands to himself.

It was amazing.

"Good to hear."

"Thanks, Boss."

"He likes you." Rockette—whose real name was Kit, which was short for Christopher—was fussing with his eye makeup in the mirror.

What did that mean? "I guess I'm lucky?"

"He was actually worried. He asked Danny if you needed help...he doesn't do that for everyone. A few, but not everyone."

"Well, I'm fine." He worked hard, and Aaron was good to him. "You need some help with your lashes?"

Kit spun around on his stool. "Could you? I've been fussing with these things forever. All I'm doing is making my eyes water."

"Well, that's no good—then they won't stick." He didn't wear false lashes as a cowboy, but a couple of the other guys did. "Dry those eyes and let them rest a minute."

Kit leaned back in his chair and let him fuss, and he had them stuck in place in no time. "There. Gorgeous."

"Thanks. I was getting ready to tear them to bits." Kit blinked a few times, looking at himself in the mirror.

"They're a pain." He settled in his chair and put his feet up. Maybe he could close his eyes for a little while before his shift.

"Hey, can I ask you something?"

He looked over at Kit, who just turned twenty-two and looked it. He'd had a lot of questions at twenty-two. "Sure."

"Are you really dating a guest?"

Oh, great. He was a rumor now. He glanced over at Jesse, who was sitting a few stations down and pretending not to listen. "I'm dating someone that comes in here sometimes, yes."

"And you met him here?"

"Why does it matter?" He didn't mean to sound so defensive, but he did kind of feel that way. It seemed like everyone was against his relationship with Teague.

"Sorry. Never mind." Kit picked up an eyebrow pencil and looked back at the mirror.

Jason sighed, but it was just as well. He didn't want to be answering a bunch of questions about Teague or their relationship; it was nobody's business.

He was wound up after that, and he didn't get any rest. He watched Kit put on eyeliner and lipstick to finish off his look, then wiggle into fishnets, a gold *lamé* tailcoat, and a matching little top hat. Kit left the dressing room in heels that Jason would have killed himself trying to take three steps in and that made Kit's legs look ten feet long. He was so impressed.

He looked at himself in the mirror.

Time to cowboy up.

After Kit's questions, he was glad Teague wasn't coming to hang out tonight. Maybe they needed to discuss it; maybe Teague shouldn't come around so much anymore. Jason would miss him, though. He liked knowing Teague was watching, it made him feel sexy and...loved.

Yeah, that was stupid maybe, but knowing Teague wanted to be there for him did make him feel loved. If that meant he had low standards, screw it. They were high enough for his man.

But Teague had an office thing tonight. A summer party that was employees only. To be honest, he'd wondered at first whether that was the truth or if Teague just didn't want him there, but he'd barely had time to worry about it. Teague had handed him the invitation, printed on fancy card stock and stamped with the firm name. Right at the bottom it said, "No guests, please" embossed in gold.

Teague was the real deal. He was straight up, both honest and truthful, totally in love, and Jason was the luckiest fake cowboy on the planet.

Jason tugged on his shorts, grateful that the weather had cooled off a little this week. He'd used a ton of powder in the last month to cut through all the humidity, but today they slid right on. He pulled on socks and stomped into his boots, buttoned his shirt up just so, and tucked his hat onto his head.

"Yeehaw," he said to the cowboy in the mirror. "Let's do this, Dallas."

"Knock 'em dead, cowboy." Jesse, who wasn't hanging on Jackson for once, gave him a big grin and a high five as he left the dressing room.

Just like every Saturday night, the club was packed. He took a second to let the music get into his body before stepping out into the crowd; then he was all smiles and swagger for the next two hours. His spotlight came up at nine as always, and he'd picked an adorable local in a Nine Inch Nails T-shirt to kiss this time.

It was a chaste kiss as always, and when Jason let the guy go, his buddies pounced on him and teased him, making the kid blush.

Keith had just helped him off the bar when a commotion broke out near the back. Jackson was working over there tonight, but Keith ran to check it out all the same.

Well, shit. What now? Should he stop? Should he keep going?

The music hadn't stopped, so he pretended like nothing was going on and did his best to draw everyone's attention back onto the dance floor. It worked, and after a minute or so, he was in the zone and watching those bills pile up on stage.

Someone moved up to the front of the stage and waved to get his attention. It was Aaron, and as soon as their eyes met, his boss made a rolling gesture with his fingers. Another song. Something was up.

He told himself he had a job to do, so he did it. The next song came on, and it wasn't one of his; it was Kit's. He understood what Aaron needed now, but he was worried about his friend. He improvised as best he could, making a

Broadway tune as sexy as he could manage. He'd laugh about this later, right? He hoped so.

When the song finally ended, he gathered up his cash and gave the crowd a wave. Things seemed to have settled down until he got backstage and saw Jackson getting stitches from an EMT over a bruised eye that was swollen shut.

"Jesus Christ, Jackson. What happened? Where's Kit?"

"Jason, can you go?"

"Can I...?"

Aaron got right in his face. "In the ambulance with Kit. Go with him, call me as soon as you know something."

"Ambulance? Is he okay?" He was trying to keep up, but he suddenly felt terrified and overwhelmed.

"No. And he can't be alone. I'll pay you, don't worry. Please go."

"Jesus, Aaron. I don't care about the money. I'll go."

"I know. That's why I'm sending you. Call me."

Two burly EMTs rolled a stretcher past him with Kit strapped onto it. Kit's head and neck were immobilized, and his face was battered and swollen.

Jesus Christ. That was terrifying. He looked at Aaron and nodded once. "Let me get my phone. I'm going. I'll call." He dug his phone out of his bag, tossed Aaron his hat and ran out after the stretcher.

15

"So, what's happening with the Avenstone deal?"

Teague looked up, surprised to see Carson standing there. "Are you talking to *me*?"

Carson snorted. "Okay. I deserve that, I've been a little standoffish."

A little standoffish? Carson had been shooting him looks and not speaking to him for weeks. Fortunately, Teague had been too busy to worry about it. "Just a little."

"You hurt my feelings. It was hard to swallow."

"Carson I—" Thankfully, Carson interrupted him, because he wasn't sure what he'd been about to say. He didn't want to be having this conversation here. Or at all.

"It's cool. I assumed and you know what they say about that. I was rude, presumptuous, all of that stuff. So we can drop it and move forward. Deal?"

Well, that was interesting. Maybe Carson had a contrite bone after all. "Yes. Deal." He held up his Coke, and Carson clinked glasses with him.

"So...Avenstone?"

"It's almost done. We're really close to closing. The

researchers' new counsel re-engineered the deal, Avenstone pushed back gently on a couple of issues, but those were minor in context. They're delivering a final agreement next week." If everything looked good, which he expected it would, then after that it was just about signatures and money.

"Sounds great. Congrats."

"Thanks." He sipped his soda and waited. He'd put money on what Carson would say next, but he had no one to bet but Carson himself.

"Heard anything about a promotion?"

Bingo. There it was. Damn it, he could have been a rich man.

"Possibly? Bucky mentioned that he wants to talk after the closing."

"It's Bucky now, hm?"

Teague shook his head. "It was William, until William sat me down last week and said, 'Call me Bucky.' So...now I do." It was awkward, though, a little like growing up and calling your high school best friend's parents by their first names. It felt disrespectful. But it seemed more disrespectful not to do what Will—*Bucky*—had asked him to.

He knew saying it would get a rise out of Carson, and he'd be lying if he didn't admit he was smug about that. It meant Carson wasn't the golden boy anymore and knew it.

"What are you working on?"

"Oh." Carson stalled by sipping his drink. "So." He stalled longer by finishing it off and shaking the ice around in the glass as if he might find more. "I'm between deals right now, but I'm working on it."

He nodded and was about to say something sympathetic when Carson went on.

"I've closed four deals since January, though, so I'm on

schedule on my hours." Carson grinned at him. "I'm going to get another drink, you want something?"

Hell, no. He was honoring his promise to himself to never drink at another office function when Carson was in attendance. "No thanks, I'm good." Plus, Carson was being a smug bastard, and he didn't have time for that nonsense.

"Okay." Carson took two steps away and turned back. "You look great, by the way."

Oh, you sly fucking dog.

Carson was working on him again. And he'd fallen for it. *Damn it.*

He made his way over to the patio. The party was being held at a rooftop venue in Tribeca and the view was spectacular, especially right now as it neared sunset. There was a partial view of the river, enough to see the orange sun setting over the water, dipping low with New Jersey in silhouette.

He took a picture for himself and decided to take a selfie to send to Jason. He turned his back to the railing and lucked into a perfect shot of the sun reflecting in the water and a not-too-dorky smile.

Carson was right; he did look pretty good, if he could say so himself. Dressing for an office end-of-summer party was a lot more complicated than it seemed. He'd had to go shopping for a shirt that didn't say "work" but didn't say "collegiate beach bum" either. With Jason's help, Teague had found a printed short-sleeved dress shirt that he liked, dark blue with a light diamond pattern on it, and wore it with his best business-casual khakis and a pair of brown loafers.

No socks. Not his favorite look, but Jason said it was right, and he was living dangerously.

He couldn't invite Jason to this party; it was employees only and no one had dates. He was going to get Jason dressed up for something in the near future, though. Something amazing with dancing and a view even better than this one...maybe a dinner cruise or reservations at a swanky restaurant. It probably wasn't Jason's scene, but he wanted to spoil his lover a little. And guests were invited to the winter holiday party, so he'd bring Jason to that one.

He sent off the selfie and a short "Wish you were here." He liked the other attorneys in the firm just fine and was friendly with them, but he was going to get bored soon. He wasn't going to hang out with this crowd once dinner was over, the alcohol really started flowing and the dancing began. That was always when Carson came sniffing around. Every damn time. But not tonight. He was going to make it an early night, go home and call Jason, and avoid any potential confrontation with Carson.

He was taken now. Exclusive. He had a lover who appreciated him. Life was pretty damn good.

This place is great. Beautiful view, boring party. Still on for brunch tomorrow?

He didn't get a reply, but he didn't expect one yet. Jason was working and wouldn't have his phone on him.

Jason was always telling him how he made crazy good money on Saturdays, mostly from tourists in from all over the country. The Midwesterners were the most polite but tipped the worst, the southerners were dirtier but more fun and good for the money....Teague knew more about the exotic dancing industry than he'd ever wanted to know.

But truthfully, he tried not to think about it too hard. He wasn't typically the jealous type, but all those eyes on Jason's body made his skin crawl a little if he let himself go there. It was better when he was actually at the bar...it was easier to believe that it was just a game when he could see for himself that it was all a show. Even watching Jason take men back for lap dances was somehow easier than knowing it was going on when he wasn't there.

So, he just didn't let himself think too hard.

Much.

Besides, his lover had been honest with him from the beginning. Jason needed the job, and he enjoyed the work. He made great money. That was pretty much the textbook definition of a successful career, wasn't it? Teague tried very hard to respect that.

Very hard.

"Teague?"

He blinked and looked over at Barb. "Oh, hey."

"I know you're not drunk an hour into this shindig."

"No." Teague laughed, embarrassed. "I'm not, I was off on a...mental boondoggle." He waved his hand vaguely at the scenery.

"Easy to do, looking at this view."

"It's gorgeous."

"There's food out now, you should see the spread. The theme may be barbecue but it's not the burgers and dogs I'm used to for sure." Barb grinned. "Try the ribs, they're amazing."

"I'll do that. Are you having a good time?"

"I love these things. I just float from group to group, listening. Either nobody ever seems to notice I'm there, or they've had enough to drink they aren't filtering around me. It's fascinating."

Teague laughed. "You're a riot, Barb. What are you drinking?"

"Sprite."

"Ah, I like your strategy. Stay sober while the rest of us drink."

"You're not drinking. You've been nursing that soda for an hour."

"You're observant." Shit, she had to know about Carson, then. "I've decided drinking at these things is bad for me."

"Smart move, Boss." She winked at him.

Oh, God. She totally knew. "Is this extortion or blackmail?" He was joking. Hopefully she was too.

Barb laughed. "Oh, Teague. It's none of my business is what it is, but you know how I feel about Carson. You need someone who doesn't look at you like a mirror."

He blinked at her. That was so well said. "You're sharp, Barb." He leaned sideways and lowered his voice. "I'm seeing someone else. I'm very taken, no worries."

Barb's eyes lit up. "You are? That's great. Also none of my business, but great."

"No, it's okay. It's an official thing, it's not a secret."

"Oh, excellent. Tell me about him?"

That was the million-dollar question, wasn't it? Where should he start? He shrugged at Barb. "He's kind, he's hot, he's funny. He takes good care of me." All true. And avoiding the hot-button issue.

"Aw, he sounds sweet. Where did you meet him? How long have you been seeing each other?"

"We met at a bar in Hell's Kitchen about...six weeks ago I guess?" He hadn't been counting. It was a hot time. Steaming hot.

"Nice. Do you have a picture?"

A presentable one? "Maybe? Let me check."

"Maybe?" Barb laughed. Teague tried not to blush and failed.

He scrolled through his recent pics. God, all his pics of Jason were either pin-up style or bordering on X-rated. It was time for some PG selfies. "Oh. Here." He found one with

Jason in shorts and a T-shirt and only looking a little mussed. He showed his phone to Barb.

"Oh, he's adorable. Young, huh?"

"He's not that much younger than I am; he just looks young." Jason did have a bit of a baby face.

"Well. Good for you, Teague. I hope it works out, you're a good man. You deserve it."

"Thanks, Barb. That's surprisingly kind, coming from the Queen of Snark." He grinned at her.

"Go get dinner before I quit on you."

"Oh. Don't do that!" He laughed, taking a few steps away. "I'm going...I'm going."

Barb winked at him and he went inside.

She was right, the food was fantastic. He had the ribs as she'd suggested and wasn't disappointed. He had some shrimp and some tiny little crab cakes. It was definitely not the barbecue he grew up with.

By the time he was done eating it was dark out, and the scenery had changed completely. The city was lit up and gorgeous, geometric lights against a purple sky. He took another picture and started to send it to Jason when a whole string of texts came scrolling in at once.

Bad night. I'm fine. At the hospital with Kit.

Someone beat him up.

Gave Jackson a black eye and stitches.

I'M FINE. Don't worry.

Are you there? Jason had been texting him for more than an hour.

Teague stared at his phone as all of it registered. His fingers started flying as he texted Jason. *Hey. Just got your texts. Call me.*

He paced a little, anxiously watching his phone and waiting for an answer. *Shit, shit, shit.*

He wasn't panicking, not really, but it didn't sound good, and he knew without being asked that Jason definitely needed him. He decided he'd better start saying his good-byes. As soon as Jason replied, he was getting in an Uber.

"Excuse me? I'm sorry, this is a private party." Carson's voice carried across the room and he turned and saw Carson put a hand out to stop Jason from getting any farther.

Jason?

"Wait, I know you." Carson blinked. "Dallas, right? The boots gave you away. Or maybe it was the obscenely tiny cutoffs."

"Jason." He excused himself from his colleagues and hurried over. "Jesus, are you okay?"

Jason rushed into his arms. "I couldn't reach you. I needed to see you. You didn't text me back..." His lover was talking a mile a minute, frantic and worried.

The music was still playing, people were still dancing. If he could get Jason out now, this would be no big deal.

Except there was Carson. "What's this about?"

"Nothing, Carson." He dismissed Carson with a wave. "Let it go, okay? He had a bad night." He led Jason outside where it was quieter and more private.

Carson followed.

"What is he—hold up, Teague. What am I seeing here?" Carson laughed darkly. "Teague. Is this the guy you've been seeing? *This* guy? A fucking cheap whore exotic dancer?"

Teague shoved away a spike of anger and stared at Carson, keeping his voice low. "What did you say?"

Carson snorted, grinning like he was on to something. "Whoa, Teague. What are you going to do? Hit me? Over *that*?" Carson pointed right at Jason.

"Oh. Oh, wow. Okay, Teague. Let's just go, okay?" Jason's

cool fingers touched him lightly on the arm. "He's not worth it."

"You are," he said with a growl, leaning toward Carson. He was already worried about Jason. He didn't need much convincing to take Carson down.

"Go on, hit me. I dare you, Teague," Carson taunted, voice barely above a whisper. "Hit me in front of all these people. Make an even bigger scene. You've already got some explaining to do—you ready to kiss that partnership good-bye?"

He narrowed his eyes, fingers balling into fists. It was time to go, he knew that. Carson was baiting him again; hitting him was just what the man wanted him to do. Make a scene, make a mess for himself. He wouldn't do it. "Shut your mouth, Carson."

"Come on, baby." Jason was tugging on his arm now and he took a step backward, letting Jason lead him away.

"I'm so fucking impressed by your date, Teague. Do you get a discount on the lap dances?"

Teague stopped moving but Jason grabbed him with both hands, pulling hard. "No. No, baby. Not him, not here. You come on, now. Come with me."

He listened because he trusted Jason and because Jason needed him more than he needed to fix this right now. He was angry and not thinking clearly. Jason looped an arm through his and he nodded and said good night to anyone who looked his way as they left, trying very hard to ignore the looks. He'd deal with that another day. They stepped into the elevator, but once the doors closed, he lost it. "Mother*fucker*!" He kicked the doors. "That should have been his fucking head!" he shouted, angrily.

"Don't. Please? I just...can't right now." Jason's hands

were on him still, stroking over his arms now, down his chest.

He looked at Jason and tried to breathe. The anger cooled quickly as he looked into his lover's eyes, only to be replaced by horror and shame. He pulled Jason close. "Are you okay?"

"Yes," Jason answered, but he shook his head no and leaned on Teague hard.

"God, I'm so sorry. I-I'm sorry about that."

"It's not your fault he's a dick."

Teague sighed. "Still. He was a dick to you. And I wanted to—" He started to make another fist and he stopped talking. He'd wanted to flatten Carson's smug, disrespectful face. But he also wanted to know what was going on with his lover. "Why are you here? What happened at the hospital? Are you sure you're okay?"

Jason sighed, words muffled in Teague's shirt. "Kit's new boyfriend showed up and beat him up in the back room."

Oh, fuck.

That was probably every bit as bad as it sounded. "Jesus. And put him in the hospital?"

Jason nodded.

"How is he doing?"

"Better. Well, he'll be there a couple of nights, I guess. Danny's going to stay with him tonight."

"And the boyfriend?"

Jason shrugged. "He got into it with Jackson, and Jackson nearly killed him. He'll be in the hospital a while too."

"Good." What else was there to say? Jason needed to know whose side he was on.

"I'm sorry I crashed the party. I texted you, but you didn't answer me. I shouldn't have come, I wasn't thinking straight. I was just really upset and...I'm sorry."

"Hey, it's okay. I wasn't getting cell service inside during dinner, and I didn't get your texts until I went back outside afterward. By then—" It was too late to text.

"I was here?"

"Yeah."

"Shit." Jason's hand slipped into his as they stepped out onto the sidewalk.

"It wouldn't have been a big deal if Carson had just minded his own damn business." But of course, Carson was a few drinks in, which amplified his asshole tendencies. Jason's outfit might have turned a few heads, but all of this could have been much simpler.

"Is this okay? Are you going to get in trouble?"

He sighed and rubbed his face. "Who the hell knows? No, I shouldn't. All you did was show up, and we left. At least Carson had the sense to keep his voice down."

"And you didn't hit him."

"I didn't." He found a grin for Jason. "I wanted to. You didn't let me."

"You've already bruised your knuckles for me. I know you can. You don't have to stand up to everyone that calls me a whore."

He stared at Jason. "Yeah, I do. That's bullshit. It's rude and disgusting."

Jason shrugged. "Baby, in my line of work, you might hear it a lot."

"And I'll get pissed off every time."

"Why?"

"Because you're not a whore, Jason. What do you mean?"

"I mean what are you worried about?" Jason looked at

him sidelong. "That they think I'm a whore or that they think you're dating a whore?"

"What?" He stopped walking, tugged Jason to the curb where they would be out of the way, and took a deep breath. He must have gotten lost in this conversation somewhere. This was supposed to be about Jason not about him. God, he was confused. "Did I do something wrong? Are you upset with me?"

"No. It's just a question."

"It's not just a question. You're asking me if I care more about you, or about how things look."

Jason put a hand on his chest. "Why were you so angry?"

He looked down at Jason, held his lover's eyes. "I was pissed because Carson is a rude fucking asshole who called the man I love a whore."

Jason's eyes went wide and for a second he looked like he might pass out, but then the look changed into something softer, and Jason smiled. "I love you too."

Oh. Had he never said that out loud before? "I mean that. If I haven't said it, I do love you."

"You haven't said it." Jason smiled and went up on his toes for a kiss.

"I love you." Teague caught Jason's chin in his fingers and kissed him gently, tangling their tongues together. "There. Now I have."

"I'm the luckiest man ever." Jason blinked at him slowly, as if he were a little drunk.

Teague felt pretty smug about that and smiled at him. "That's my line."

"I'm sorry I ruined your evening."

He combed his fingers through Jason's thick hair. "Does it feel ruined?"

That won him a bright smile. "No. It feels great."

"Every moment is better with you in it."

Jason didn't ask for a kiss this time, he just took it, so hard it forced Teague to back up a step. He dove right in, answering that kiss with everything in his heart that he needed Jason to know. He could stand here on this corner and make out with Jason forever. It didn't matter who was looking. Maybe he'd lost his mind, but he didn't care if Carson or anyone else thought he was crazy.

He could lose his mind; he'd found his heart.

16

"Is he okay?"

Jason was wearing one of his shirts again. It was a black T-shirt this time, and Teague watched him as he talked on the phone, leaning against the kitchen counter, looking absolutely edible.

He was probably going to get a phone call today, or be called into someone's office on Monday, but right now he didn't care. He was happy. Jason was here with him.

"Yeah, I have his rings and stuff. A chain he had around his neck. I didn't want to leave them. I'll keep them safe until he gets home. Is he talking?"

Is he talking? Jesus, what had this boyfriend of Kit's done? He glanced over at his lover as he scrambled eggs. Jason had been exhausted by the time they got back to his place and hadn't felt like talking, so Teague had let it be, got him showered, and tucked him in.

He thought about how good Jason looked in his bed: fair skin and blond curls against his black sheets. So beautiful. But it was more than that. Jason looked comfortable. Happy. He looked like he belonged there.

"Okay. When is his brother coming up?"

Oh, the kid had family. Good.

"Yeah. I can come sit with him tomorrow. Call me before you leave the hospital tonight....Okay. Thanks, Danny. Bye."

Jason tapped his phone to end the call and set it down on the counter.

"How is he?"

Jason shrugged. "Awake. Danny says he's bruised and swollen, but the X-rays show it looks worse than it is. He's lucky."

"Did I hear he has family on the way?"

Jason nodded. "His brother is driving up from North Carolina tomorrow. Kit will probably go home with him."

"And the boyfriend?" He pulled the bacon out of the oven.

"Jackson did a number on him. He's still unconscious."

"Good." *Asshole.* "Then Kit can get away before he wakes up."

"Yeah. He'll be safe with his brother." Jason pulled the bacon off the pan, layered it on a plate, and topped off their coffees while he finished up the eggs.

"You want cheese?"

"No, thanks."

They moved around each other easily and quietly, putting all the food on the table and settling down to eat.

"Mm. Good eggs, baby. Thank you." Jason smiled at him over his fork.

He reached for a piece of bacon, playing this cool. "So... what about you?" he asked as casually as he could manage.

"Me?" Jason's eyes flicked up from his plate.

"Yes. How are you feeling?"

Jason waved at him with his fork. "Me? I'm fine."

"Are you?"

"Of course."

He reached for Jason, touching the back of his lover's hand. "You seemed pretty freaked out last night."

Jason pulled his hand away and forked up a bite of eggs. "Well, it was weird that's all. There was all this chaos, and it was Kit's set and I had to cover. Then Aaron sent me with him....I wasn't expecting my night to go like that is all."

"Jason." He got Jason's attention and held it. "You crashed my party to find me. You were scared."

Jason looked away. "I was worried."

"Yeah?" He wanted Jason to keep talking. "I get that. I'll tell you what it made me think of—"

"Don't, Teague."

He ignored that and continued. "That guy that was waiting for you outside the club. The one you called Chicago."

"That was different." Jason's tone was dismissive, but Teague caught the emotion in Jason's voice.

"How? Someone showed up, got aggressive with Kit, and the bouncers had to step in. That Chicago guy was just as dangerous, he just had less opportunity."

"He wasn't my boyfriend."

"That makes it better? That it was a stranger?"

"Well, my boyfriend hits other people for me." Jason grinned, flirting, trying to distract him.

"What if Chicago comes back?"

Jason shook his head. "He won't."

"How do you know?"

"I don't. But I can't worry about that, Teague. Okay?" Jason set his fork down and looked out the window.

"You have to."

"No. I won't do that. I can't be paranoid all the time, I

won't—" Jason bit his lips together and stopped talking abruptly.

"Won't what?"

Jason looked at him, eyes worried. "Can't we just eat breakfast?"

"Sorry. Yes." He took Jason's hand and kissed the long fingers. "Have you tried the bacon?" He'd try to let it go for a little while, but they were into it now, and they needed to finish this conversation.

They ate, but it was mostly quiet as they looked out the window and watched the city go by several stories below them. Jason asked about the party—the rest of it—but that got awkward quickly too as they avoided discussing Carson. It wasn't until they started cleaning up, shoulder to shoulder in front of the kitchen sink, that Jason finally started talking again.

"I can't think too hard about what happened to Kit or think about that guy coming back. If I do, if I start to get worried, I won't want to go there anymore."

He nodded. Jason hadn't looked at him yet, so Teague kept his eyes on the dishes. "Well, maybe you don't need to."

"Teague." Jason sighed, and he could read the disappointment in those shoulders.

"I know, I know. I'm sorry. I just want you safe." And it was looking more and more to him like this could be a dangerous career choice.

"It's the first job I've ever really liked, Teague. Ever."

"I understand. But you could find something..." He threw caution to the wind and just said what he'd been thinking. "I mean if you didn't have to worry about the money, or rent...maybe something similar?"

"If I didn't have to worry about money? Baby, life is

worrying about money. Daily. I work, I get paid, I pay my rent. Or I don't, and I'm crashing on someone's couch or on the street. That's my reality."

"It's not anymore."

Jason glanced at him, then put down the towel he'd been using to dry dishes and wandered off toward the living room, leaving him standing there alone.

Shit. Was Jason mad? He hadn't stormed off, but he didn't seem thrilled with Teague's suggestion either. Was he insulted? Maybe he just needed to think. Maybe he didn't want to talk about it. Maybe...

Go after him, idiot.

Right. Usually he hated that voice in his head that always thought he was stupid, but right now it was pretty on point.

He dried his hands and went off in Jason's wake. Teague followed Jason's lead in other ways too and didn't rush, but when he spotted his lover tucked into a corner of his couch, he went right over and sat beside him.

After a silent minute. Jason turned toward him and took his hand. That was good, right? Holding hands was good.

"We joked that night we met at the bar that you were a heartbreaker, remember?"

"And that yours had been broken a hundred times." He nodded. He remembered every detail about that night, it was the night he met his soul mate.

"Well, it hasn't. Not a hundred times. Only once, really."

His last man had a little money too, and that turned out badly. Danny's words came back to him, putting things in sudden, sharp focus.

Damn it. He shouldn't have—

"His name was Simon. He was an investment banker."

Jason's gaze was vague and unfocused, eyes looking down at the rug or the coffee table. "He was handsome, he gave me gifts and attention."

"You were in love with him?"

"I was." Jason nodded. "I was very in love and he broke my heart, for real."

"Yeah. Danny told me it didn't end well."

Jason's eyes snapped over to him. "Danny told you?"

"Not details." He smoothed a hand over Jason's arm to calm him. "Just that the guy had some money and it ended badly. That's it."

Jason sighed, nodding. "Yeah, that's true. He had money, he courted me for a while, then he asked me to move in."

He rolled his eyes and sighed. "Fuck, I'm sorry. I..." He wanted to say something in his defense: *I didn't know, I'm sincere, I love you more than anyone.* But he shut his mouth and let Jason talk. There was time for that. It wasn't about him right now. "Go ahead, sorry."

Jason squeezed his hand and smiled. "You're good. You're so good to me."

"So, he asked you to move in?"

"He did, and I agreed. I spent every dime I had to move my shit and pay off the last of my rent."

He could read the tension settling into Jason's shoulders and knew this was going to get complicated fast. He didn't want to interrupt, so he touched Jason's face instead, running his fingers along Jason's jaw, just letting his lover know he was listening.

"I was there for a couple of months. It was wonderful mostly, domestic bliss and all of that. Saturday errands, lazy Sundays. And then one day it just...took this awful turn."

He frowned. "What happened?"

Jason shrugged. "He got short-tempered, started coming home late. He kept bringing up money when he knew I didn't have any. I couldn't do anything right. I asked him one night if he was seeing someone else, and he tried to hit me."

"Jesus."

"He didn't. I was faster than he was. He said he was sorry but...he wasn't sorry. Maybe he was sorry he asked me to move in. Or that he couldn't bring his new boy toy home. Who knows? I called Ricky and we grabbed everything we could while he was at work the next day, and I moved back into the apartment in Brooklyn."

"You have good friends."

"I do. Ricky even said he'd missed me."

He held off on his questions, and it was hard not to insist he wasn't like that, that Jason would be safe with him. That money didn't matter. True or not, Jason had something to work out and an understandable fear.

It sucked to try to live up to a lesson learned, though.

"So...I've struck a nerve, I see." He grinned and kissed Jason's temple.

Jason laughed gently. "A little."

"I just love you," he said simply.

"I love you too. It's not about whether this is real. I know it is."

"Okay. I'm not going anywhere. I'm stubborn that way." Something still wasn't making sense to him.

"Simon had a good job, money. He asked me to move in and I did. I worked a little, but he didn't need me to, he paid for everything. He—" Jason shook his head. "I want to keep my job, Teague."

"Jason—"

"I don't know what actually prompted this, but if I move

in with you, then I don't need it. Right? That's what you were saying?"

Fuck. How could he talk his way out of that one? "Well, I—"

Jason's eyes narrowed.

"Okay. Yes. I was thinking you would be safer not working there."

"I like my job, baby. I know you're probably upset that I showed up last night dressed like—I dress at work. I embarrassed you, right? I'm sorry but—"

"No. What? No." He wasn't embarrassed. He was worried about Jason and pissed at Carson.

"It's okay, I hear what you're saying."

"No. No, you're not hearing me at all. You're not hearing me because I've been letting you talk. So, hear me now. I'm *not* embarrassed. You don't have a conventional job, and maybe that's strange to some people. Okay, fine. But my only motivation in asking you to move in was to keep you safe."

"To keep me."

"Keep you *safe*, Jason. Not *kept*. Kept safe. Don't put words in my mouth."

"Are you jealous?"

"Am I—" He sat back and stared at Jason. "Why do you pick fights with me all the time? I'm not jealous. I'm worried. I love you, and I'm worried about you. Jesus Christ, Jason. Shoot me for wanting to take care of you."

Jason stood and stalked a few steps away. "I don't want to be taken care of or paid for. I don't want a jealous lover. I want to keep my job, and I want you to be okay with that."

He stood as well, just to pace and get his thoughts straight. He wasn't following where Jason was going. He didn't understand it. "I'm not jealous. I'm not trying to wrap you in bubble wrap. I'm not conditioning this relationship on moving in with me, on whether you keep or quit your job." He stopped pacing and looked at Jason again. "I'm feeling...accused. Like I've done something wrong. I'm sorry you have a shitty history with some banker that wanted a trophy more than he wanted you, but I'm not that guy. I'm not. You don't want me to look after you, fine. That's up to you. Maybe I need you more than you need me. I can accept that. But please don't write me off because I think taking care of someone is part of the privilege of being in love."

"Teague."

"Look. The offer is open. Keep your job and move in whenever you feel like you want to. If you don't ever want to, well...well, I'll be disappointed, but I won't love you any less." He was upset now, and he didn't want to be. Jason was scared, he got it. "I'm not sorry I brought it up."

Jason moved toward him and hugged him, and Teague exhaled, letting the tension out as he circled his arms around his lover. Jason needed to push sometimes, he was learning that. He didn't like that this one felt like a test, but maybe that was what Jason needed. Maybe Jason needed him to pass and to not be like that other guy that just wanted something pretty.

"I love you." Jason's hand pushed into his sweats, and he gasped at the unexpected touch and the way his body lit up, responding as if Jason had found an on switch.

"Jason."

"Shh."

He wasn't asking for—he didn't—*oh, fuck*. "What are—"

"Shut up, Counselor."

"Okay. Yeah." He sucked in a breath and his nipples went hard and tight as Jason found one with his teeth. "Fuck."

"You're hot when you're mad."

He growled. He wasn't mad; he was upset. And now he was horny as hell. He pushed his stiffening cock through Jason's fingers, the touch just perfect. Jason hummed and shoved him onto the couch and tugged his sweats down and over his ankles.

"You don't have—"

"Jesus, baby. Shut up and let me blow you." Jason knelt on the floor between Teague's thighs.

"Yes. Okay. Fuck, yes." What a pretty sight that was. Jason cupped his balls, sending lightning through his veins, and his eyes crossed. "Oh, God."

Jason's mouth closed over the head of his erection and he shivered. His hands fumbled uselessly for a moment; then he got control of himself, tangled one in Jason's hair, and hooked the other over the back of the sofa.

Jason's mouth was heaven on earth, but his tongue was evil incarnate and between the two, Jason managed to drive Teague out of his mind. He was panting and moaning shamelessly, hips lifting off the couch, toes curling into the carpet. He'd been wound up to start with, and now he felt like he was ready to explode. He was burning for this. Lit up like a Roman candle that Jason had ignited with a blowtorch. But Jason kept him hovering on the edge for so long he was ready to beg.

Fuck it. He did. "Please, baby. Fuck, so good. I need—"

Jason took his aching cock down his throat and swallowed, and he went supernova, stars and light dancing and blinding him as he shook and shot hard.

"Mm." Jason hummed, that evil tongue turned gentle as it made its way over his abs and across his chest until it found his lips.

Teague drew Jason into his lap, still sucking in deep gulps of air around their kiss. He was sure there was something else he should be thinking about, but Jason's lips, warm hands, and hard body were all he cared about right now. He tugged the waistband of Jason's briefs down to free his beautiful, hard cock and gripped it tight.

"Teague!" Jason gasped and humped right up into his touch.

He jacked Jason hard and fast, listening to Jason's needy sounds and rough grunts. Jason tossed his head back, arching into his hand and he swooped his thumb over the head again and again, spreading hot fluid everywhere his fingers touched. Jason started to tremble and groan, fingers digging into his shoulders.

"T-Teague. Baby. Gonna."

"Yeah." He knew. "So beautiful. Love how you move. How you smell. Let me watch you come."

Jason soaked his fist and abs with a shiver and a shout. He loosened his grip and stroked his lover through it, milking to the very last drop and then some, until Jason was a relaxed puddle in his lap.

"Take me to bed?"

He huffed a laugh. "My pleasure." They could clean up later.

Jason wasn't moving in or leaving his job. It wasn't ideal —Teague still wished he could keep Jason safe, but he had a compromise in mind, and he'd bring it up after their nap. Jason had shared something very personal with him, and he'd been as honest as he knew how to be. He felt good about where they'd left things mostly, like they had a deeper emotional connection. The more visceral connection had eased him, and hopefully Jason too. He led Jason to the bedroom.

"Climb on in and let me hold you."

"There's nowhere I'd rather be." Jason stripped out of his T-shirt and settled in the sheets.

Teague pulled the curtains closed against the bright morning sun and crawled into bed with his lover.

17

The view out of the window in Kit's room wasn't half bad. Jason looked down at the rooftops of shorter buildings and out over the city, trying to catch signs of life—of people working in buildings or wandering around on rooftop patios. It didn't make him feel better about being here—he still hated hospitals—but if he had to be, this room was all right.

"Not a bad view, huh?" Kit's voice startled him.

He turned around and made himself smile for Kit when all he wanted to do was wince. Everything about Kit looked painful. "Hey. I thought you were asleep."

"Dozing. The pain meds make me kind of dizzy."

"Let me get you some water. Your throat sounds dry." He walked over to the little plastic pitcher by the bed, poured a cup, and stuck the straw in it. Kit drank the whole cup, so he poured a little more.

"Thank you. I was thirsty."

"Pain meds do that too."

Kit nodded and looked over at him. "This sucks. Thank you for being here."

"You're welcome. I don't want you to be alone right now. That would be even worse." Hospitals were awful places.

"Have you heard anything about Jackson? Is he okay?"

He laughed, remembering his conversation with Aaron this morning. "Yeah. Aaron says he's wearing the stitches over his eye like he earned them. He thinks they make him look badass. He's totally fine." They probably stung a little, but it didn't sound like Jackson cared at all.

"He looks badass anyway." Kit grinned at him.

That was the truth. "I think so, yeah."

"How's your man? Are things okay?"

Jason blinked at the question. "Yeah, things are good." A little awkward yesterday with the whole "moving in" talk, but good. "He asked me to move in. I said no. The usual craziness."

"Gary asked me to quit. Well, told me to quit. I told him no so he showed up to make me quit."

"That's his name? Gary?"

Kit nodded. "He was a guest, like your man."

"Gary..." He didn't know a Gary.

"He comes in during the daytime more. Works nights usually. You might not have seen him much."

"How did you find out I was dating a guest?"

"Well, there was a rumor....I wanted to talk to you about it, but you wouldn't. Remember?"

"Yeah." He nodded. He remembered now. They'd talked just before Kit's shift and Kit had questions...*shit*. "I'm sorry. If I'd known there was a reason you were asking..."

Kit waved him off. "Doesn't matter. But Danny filled me in more yesterday."

Jason sighed. "Ah. Of course he did."

"Hey, who am I going to tell? I'm not going back to work, I'm going home with my brother."

Wow. So Kit really was leaving the city. "That's the plan? For good?"

Kit shrugged. "I think so. I need a break, and my brother Jake is cool with...me."

It was good Kit had family. "Older or younger?"

"Older. He's married, has kids and a steady job and a house and the whole thing."

"He hit a home run." Jason chuckled. "It sounds so...storybook."

"It is, kind of. I'm looking forward to hanging out with my niece and nephew, taking it slow. I don't know what I'm going to do there yet but..."

"You'll figure something out, Kit. You're smart."

Kit nodded. "I hope so. It's going to be a very lonely, boring place if I don't."

The room went quiet for a minute as a nurse came in to check on Kit and start his release paper work. When she left, Kit looked at him seriously.

"You be careful with that suit of yours."

Jason nodded. "I am. But he's a good man."

"I thought Gary was a good man for a while."

Jason wasn't sure what to say to that. "I'll be careful, Kit."

Kit reached over and took his hand. "Even if he is a nice guy, guys like that, guys with money? They're heartbreakers. His wallet is always more important than you."

That wasn't true. Not Teague. But it didn't seem like Kit was going to be convinced, and honestly, Kit had been hurt and deserved to vent a little. "I'll keep my eyes open, okay? I promise. And Danny is always looking out for me."

"Good. Yes, okay." Kit squeezed his hand and let it go.

Teague's wallet was a nice feature, but it wasn't who Teague was. Teague was generous and kind and never made him feel less because he didn't have money.

Yet.

God, he hated that stupid, scared piece of him. The one that, when he was alone at night, would try to convince him he wasn't capable of making a good decision. That voice was fed and fueled by memories—of Simon: the lies Simon had told him and how little and stupid he'd felt when Simon's true colors started to show.

Teague was different.

"Hey, little brother. Whoa, you look awful. You should be in a hospital."

"Funny, Jake." Kit held his arms out and Jake gave him a careful but genuine hug.

"You ready to go home?" Jake was handsome. They looked a lot like each other, but Kit's hair was lighter, and it seemed like maybe he was a little shorter. Hard to tell with Kit in bed. Their build was about the same, and their eyes were practically interchangeable. Anyone would know they were brothers with one look.

"They're putting together the paper work. When did you get here?"

"Last night, late. I stayed in a great hotel in Midtown."

Kit rolled his eyes. "You could have stayed at my place."

"Thanks. This was easier than dealing with keys and whatever. I didn't know when I'd make it up here. The hotel was good." Jake's smile was kind. "I got room service and watched a little TV this morning. I didn't want to wake you up."

Jason stood up and offered Jake a hand. "Hi, I'm Jason."

"Jason." Jake shook, smiling. "I am so rude. I'm sorry. Nice to meet you."

He smiled. "No, you're fine. You guys have a lot of catching up to do, I bet."

"We have a long car ride for that. Would you like to get some coffee with me? I was just going to grab some."

Oh. Awkward. "Uh. I—" He looked at Kit.

"Go ahead. Bring me some?"

"Yeah, we'll do that. Come on, Jason." For some reason, Jake wasn't taking no for an answer, so Jason followed along.

"I'll be right back." Jason tapped Kit's toes on the way out.

"Do you know where the cafeteria is?"

"Yeah, I've been there a couple of times. I'll show you. Elevators are over there." He pointed and Jake led the way.

"So, did you know this Gary guy?"

Oh, boy. Questions. "Uh. No. Not at all. I didn't even know Kit was seeing him."

"What about this bar Kit was working at?"

Bar. Jake said "bar," not "club." "What about it?"

"Is it sleazy? Was Kit...was he...you know."

"It's a men's club. We dance and mingle and that's all." He got into the elevator. "That's *all*."

Jake squinted at him. "You work there too."

"Yeah."

Jake shook his head.

"Look. Kit said they were dating. He said Gary had been good to him, and he thought Gary was fine with his job. Kit didn't do anything wrong; he had a jealous boyfriend, and the guy just...snapped when Kit said he wouldn't quit."

"Dancing. That's all?"

"That's all." Lap dances were dancing, right? He didn't need to go there. He stepped off the elevator and headed right for the coffee.

"Okay. Cool. Okay." Jake sighed and Jason watched his shoulders sag. "I worry about him a lot."

"Kit's a good guy, a good friend. He's just...not like everyone else."

Jason wasn't like everyone else either.

"I just want to see him happy. I was glad to hear he was dating, but for it to turn out like this?"

"Sometimes people are just assholes."

Jake nodded. "Sometimes. I can't imagine dating someone that dances, though. I kind of get wanting him to quit. I'm not saying it's right, but I can understand how the guy might have felt—jealous, worried—I mean, do you feel safe all the time?"

All the time? No. "Most of the time, yes. Like I said, sometimes people are—"

"Dangerous. Sometimes people are dangerous. Unpredictable. Especially in those places. That's what I told Kit, not that he ever listens to me."

Jason didn't know what to say to that. He worked in one of "those places" and he liked it. He took his coffee and a cup for Kit back to the elevator.

Jake's footsteps were loud behind him. "Sorry. I'm sorry. That was rude, I just—I'm not from around here. What do I know, right? Just ignore me."

"It's fine." He wasn't trying to make friends. But now he was a little lost in his own head, thinking about what Teague had said about worrying. He'd been thinking a lot about Teague since he woke this morning—in Teague's bed.

Again.

And he'd be going there tonight after work, he knew it, because why sleep alone if he didn't have to? Why sleep without the man he was in love with?

The man who loved him. He knew it was true. Deep down, past the memories of Simon and all that hurt and shame, he knew. He just didn't know how to get around the voice that kept saying, *What if you're wrong?*

"Seriously. Everyone has to make a living. It's cool. Just be safe."

"Thanks." He told himself Jake meant well. He thought it was true.

But maybe not honest.

Damn Teague for putting that whole thing in his head. It was interesting; Teague was right. He liked that Teague noticed things, paid attention to details like that. To him, and his details.

They rode the elevator back to Kit's floor and he put the awkwardness aside as he went in with the coffee. Kit was out of bed and getting dressed.

"Hey. Do you need help?" Jason set the coffee down and reached for Kit's shirt, pretending not to notice the bruises.

"Well, I didn't think so, but...maybe?"

"Jesus, Christoph—Kit." Jake sighed. "Sorry. *Kit*. Are you okay?"

"It's ugly, right? But I'm okay, *Jacob*." Kit smiled and winked at his brother.

"Yeah. Sorry." Jake looked at Jason. "He grew up Christopher. I'm better than our parents about it, but I still fuck it up sometimes."

Kit shrugged at Jason. "He tries."

"That's the important part." Sometimes he wished he had more family, but not when things like that came up. Just being him was much easier. He finished helping Kit dress. "Hey, you. I'll miss you. Text me when you're settled? I want to hear all about it."

"I will." Kit hugged him and he hugged back carefully. "Be safe, okay? I know you said you're fine—but be careful."

He heard what Kit meant and appreciated the lack of

details. "Yeah, man. I will." He picked up his coffee. "Nice to meet you, Jake. Take care of this guy. I like him."

"Will do. Good to meet you too."

He gave a wave to Kit and had his phone out before he made it to the elevator. He texted Teague as soon as he stopped walking.

What if I moved in on a trial basis?

The reply came back a second later even though Jason knew Teague was at work. *What if I said yes?*

God, he loved the dork. *What if you didn't answer a question with a question?*

What fun would that be?

He laughed. *I'm serious!*

Me too. Yes. Keep your place, stay at mine?

Another question? Talk after work. But yes, that was what he was thinking. His rent was paid for next month anyway, and it would give the guys time to find another roommate.

I love you. Can't wait.

He sent a heart and followed it with, *I love you too.*

Truth and honesty, both.

18

"We got it done. I wasn't sure we'd get here. I appreciate your perseverance." David Rasner stood and offered his hand.

"Mr. Rasner." Teague stood as well, and shook, giving David a nod. He'd been impressed with the new firm David had hired. "Congratulations. We'll get you a full package of original documents once we've compiled them."

"Perfect. Thank you. Have a good evening everyone." David gave a nod as he left the conference room.

"Done." Kent Orsi, his client from Avenstone, breathed a huge sigh. "Teague, you've been spectacular."

He smiled, pleased by the compliment, and secretly pretty proud of himself. "Thanks, Kent. We appreciate how you've stuck with us."

"You understood Avenstone from the beginning; I couldn't imagine working with anyone else. Hang on to him, Bucky. I look forward to the next deal." Kent packed up his briefcase and shook their hands.

Bucky smiled. "We have plans for Teague, I promise."

"Good. I'll happily steal him from you otherwise."

They all laughed as Kent left, though it wasn't a preposterous idea. It happened all the time. Lots of associates went in-house for a client if they didn't make partner. Teague puffed out a breath and started cleaning up, making neat piles of each of the documents and the relevant signatures for Barb. "That was something."

"It was. You've done very well for us, Teague." Bucky pulled an envelope out of a file on the conference table. "Read this tonight. I want you to have lunch with me and Valerie tomorrow."

With Bucky and his wife? He looked at the envelope, then glanced up again. "I-I look forward to that. Thank you, sir."

Bucky held the envelope up higher for him to take.

"Oh. Right. Yes, sir. Thank you, Mister—uh. Bucky." His cheeks were on fire, but Bucky just laughed.

"Read it, think about it, and thank me tomorrow over steaks." Bucky grinned at him and patted him in the shoulder, scooped up his things, and left the conference room.

Holy shit.

Teague looked around the empty conference room. "Holy shit, it closed." He flopped into a chair feeling exhausted and giddy. The deal had closed. Signatures. Handshakes. Thank-yous. It was done. He lifted up the envelope, stared at it, and tore it open.

"I hear congratulations are in order?" Barb came in, all smiles, and looked over the piles he made. "This is everything?"

"Yep. Everything. We'll need three copies—"

"For you, Orsi, Rasner, and the file. Got it." Barb started picking up the piles, putting each in its own folder.

"Yes. Thank you."

Barb reached for the letter in his fingers. "You want me to take that?"

"Oh." He yanked it toward him. "No. No, this is… something else."

"What is it?" Barb asked, looking both curious and like she knew something he didn't.

He eyed her. "I don't know yet. I haven't read it."

"Oh. Oh! Sorry. I'll leave you to it, then. Congratulations! On the closing…" Barb hustled for the door.

"Thank you, thank you." He waited for the door to close, then opened the letter slowly and read it.

It was an offer letter for full equity partnership in the firm, effective the first of the month.

Which meant he had to sign it by tomorrow.

This wouldn't be a problem; he'd sign it right now except he thought maybe he should read all the terms first. He was a lawyer after all, and the letter was a lot longer than the re: line.

He folded the letter back up and hopped out of his chair. He couldn't wait to tell Jason. He was going to pack up, buy some champagne, and plan a little private celebration at his place for after Jason's shift. He didn't care if it would be in the middle of the night, he was looking forward to tasting champagne on his lover's lips.

"Whitaker!"

"I'm heading out, Carson." Teague sighed and kept walking. He wasn't interested in playing Carson's games right now. He'd just made it to his office when Carson caught him.

"Teague, hold up."

He didn't wait even a second and started getting his things together. "I'm getting ready to leave."

"I just wanted to say congratulations on closing your deal."

"Thanks. I'm very pleased." *If you only knew the rest of it.* He was looking forward to telling Carson about his promotion tomorrow. Or next week. Or maybe just letting the asshole find out through the grapevine.

"I bet you are."

He glanced at Carson, uncertain of the tone of that remark. "I worked hard for it."

Carson stood in his doorway. "They're letting me go."

Oh, shit. He didn't like Carson, but Teague would never have wished that on him. "Shit. I'm sorry, Carson."

"Can you believe that? You have a whore show up at an office party and get offered a promotion, and I fall just a little shy of my numbers and get laid off? What is that bullshit?"

His blood started to boil like it had the other night at the party, only Jason wasn't here to cool him off this time. He thought maybe he was glad for that. Carson had crossed that line too many times now. "I don't want to hear another word about Jason out of your filthy mouth, you understand me? And how do you know about my—"

"I mean seriously. Did anyone even say a word to you? That just rolled right off your shoulders like water off a fucking duck, man. You're incredible."

Carson was right; nobody had said a word. Not one word, in fact. He'd expected it, waited for it all weekend, and then he'd come in Monday morning, gotten right to work, and it was business as usual. Bucky hadn't even given him a sideways glance that he'd noticed.

But none of that was any of Carson's business one way or the other. He put his letter in his briefcase, closed it, and pulled it off his desk. "I'm going home now, Carson."

He walked right into Carson's fist.

The blow sent him reeling. He dropped his briefcase right before he stumbled into his desk and managed to catch himself from falling.

Teague shook his head to clear it, and just managed to figure out what was happening in time to duck a second blow. He didn't think about what he did next, he just curled his fingers into a fist, hauled his arm back, and returned the favor, shaking out his hand as Carson tripped over a guest chair and hit the floor, nose bleeding.

He sighed and reached for a box of tissues, which he dropped onto Carson's chest. "Good luck with your new endeavor," he said dryly. Then he scooped up his briefcase and left his office.

Barb caught him on the way out. "Teague? Teague your...are you okay? Your eye..."

"I'm fine, Barb. Thank you. You should see the other guy." In truth he was a little dizzy, but he kept walking to the elevator.

"Teague?" She chased after him with a napkin full of ice from the ice machine.

"No, really. You should. He's on the floor in my office." He accepted the ice and held it to his cheekbone. Fuck, this was going to hurt tomorrow.

"Carson?"

"He hit me as I was trying to leave my office. He was blocking the door."

Barb sighed. "I heard they let him go. Figures he'd take it out on you."

Teague nodded. "I hope someone follows through on that and *makes* him leave. Now."

"I'll call security. Don't you worry about a thing."

"You're the best, Barb. I don't know what I'd do without you."

Barb smiled at him. "I like you, Teague. You're a tough lawyer, and you're a good man. Congratulations on the closing. Go home and celebrate."

Maybe he was, maybe he wasn't. But he tried. And he appreciated Barb's words in any case. "Thanks, Barb—"

"Teague! We're not done." Carson shouted from his office as the elevator doors opened.

"I better go."

"I've got this. Night, Teague."

"Night, Barb. Call me if you need me."

"I won't." Barb winked at him, her grin the last thing he saw as the doors closed.

19

"It's a trial thing, Ricky. I'm going to try it for a month."

"But how will you know after a month that he's not...Simon?"

Teague wasn't Simon. Jason knew it in his soul; it was just his brain that needed a little more convincing. "I guess I won't, but I'll know *him* better. You know?" He switched his phone to his other ear as he headed uptown from the subway toward Teague's place. *His* place? Home?

"You know you'll always have a place here, Jason. Right? No matter what. We'll move you out and we'll move you back in if we need to."

He might not have any blood family left—it was just him and his mother—but he'd lucked into his chosen family: the best roommates and best friends in the world. "I hope you won't need to. I don't think you will, honestly. But you have the rent for next month, so this way you have time to find someone and I have an out if I need one."

"Teague seems like a good guy to me. Simon never tried to get to know us, didn't give a shit about your job....Teague seems different. It took a bit, but we all like him."

Jason smiled happily. "That means a lot, man. You have no idea."

"Well, it's the truth. You have some things to work out still, I'm sure. But he cares, we all see it."

Jason stopped outside Teague's building and hung out on the sidewalk to finish their conversation. "We're talking tonight. Right now, even. I'm here at his place." Whatever they needed to work out, he knew they could. Teague listened. That was big. Huge. And Jason did his best to hear Teague too.

"Good luck, man. I'm going to miss you."

"Oh, stop. We'll see each other when you visit Danny at work, and now we have an excuse to have brunch."

Ricky laughed. "We do. I love brunch. Eggs, bacon, and cocktails? Yes, please."

He laughed. "Be good, Ricky. Smooch Danny for me."

"Will do. Night, man."

"Night." He hung up with a sigh, still smiling as he looked up the side of Teague's building toward the sky.

"Going inside?"

"Huh?" Jason blinked and looked at Chrissy, who'd come out for a smoke. "Oh. Hey Chrissy. Yes. Moving in, actually."

"Oh, yeah? Good for you guys." She winked at him and lit up. "I'll make a note and get you an ID card. Just have Mr. Whitaker confirm with me tomorrow. Go on in."

"Thanks." He nodded, still grinning. "Don't mind if I do." He went inside. Skipped, maybe, or half ran. He was so excited.

And Chrissy didn't even bat an eyelash at him anymore.

"Hey, you. Come on in." Teague answered the door looking tired.

And with a black eye.

"Oh, my God. What happened to you?"

Teague chuckled and let him in, locking the door behind him. "I got a promotion offer."

"They come with black eyes now? Do you have ice? Let me get you some ice."

Teague took his hands. "I have ice. I'm fine. Carson hit me."

Jason wilted. "I'm so confused. Did you hit him first?"

"No. Come sit."

He felt totally lost. Carson hit him over a—*oh*. Oh. "Are you okay? Is your head okay? Do you want some Tylenol?"

"My head hurts a little, honestly, and I hadn't thought to take anything..."

"Sit. You sit. Let me get you—you sit." A promotion with a side of fistfight—he couldn't wait to hear the rest of that story. He sat Teague on the couch and hurried off, returning with fresh ice, a bottle of water, and some Tylenol. Once Teague was settled with the ice on his eye, he took his lover's free hand and squeezed it. "Okay. So did you close your deal?"

Teague nodded. "We closed the deal, everyone was happy. I was feeling pretty good, and things got even better. Bucky handed me an offer letter for partnership in the firm."

"Whoa!" His boyfriend was going to be a partner in a law firm. *Wow. Him. His boyfriend.* "Congratulations, baby! That's amazing. Are you happy?"

"I am. And proud, I've been working hard for this, honestly. I wanted it." Teague looked a little awed behind the fog of his headache.

"I'm proud of you too. We'll celebrate tomorrow when you're feeling better."

"I—Bucky wants to have lunch tomorrow to talk about

the offer. You think this will be a good look?" Teague pointed to his eye.

"Oh. Oh, man. Is he going to be mad?"

"So...that's the other thing. Carson was let go today."

"Carson was—oh, shit."

"Yeah."

"So that's why he—"

Teague nodded and put the ice on his eye. "I think so. He's upset that I kind of sailed past him this year. He didn't make his numbers and—he's frustrated, I get that. But he's not a team player either. And he's got bigger issues with me apparently. He shot first, I promise."

First? "You didn't hit him back, did you?"

"Yes." Teague nodded. "Once. Then I left."

Oh, no. "Teague. You shouldn't have."

"I wouldn't have if it had been over work, but...it was over you." Teague looked a little sheepish.

Jason blinked. "Me? I thought it was about the promotion?"

Teague shook his head. "He's jealous, he was trying to push my buttons, and he said some ugly things. Some of the same things he said the night of the party and I—"

"Teague." Jason sighed.

"He deserved it, Jason. And frankly, I *wanted* to hit him. I'm sorry, but I did. He's pretended to be a friend for too long. I've had it."

"But your promotion—"

"I'm pretty confident this won't affect that at all. When I left, Barb was calling security."

"Jesus." If Teague lost this promotion because of him...

"Of course, showing up with a shiner at lunch with you on my arm will certainly make an impression."

What? With him? "Wait—me?"

Teague put the ice down and tangled their fingers. "I'd like you to be there, yes."

No. No way. "I don't know anything about promotions and law firms and—oh, God. I can't go, baby."

"This is the kind of thing people bring their husbands and wives to. Lunch with the boss to celebrate a promotion. Steak, he said. Please come?"

No. No, he couldn't. God, he couldn't even imagine. "Teague, I don't understand how I haven't gotten you fired yet. Between showing up like an idiot at your office party and Carson being a dick...your boss has got to think awful things."

"I got an offer letter, didn't I? Bucky is rewarding my work and minding his own business. I'm lucky, you know? Not everyone would. I feel like we should trust him."

Jason stared at Teague. "I don't know."

"It's just lunch."

"They'll ask me what I do for a living. They'll ask me where I'm from and about my parents and...I'm not like these people."

"And you'll be honest, or you'll change the subject, or whatever you need to do. And I'll back you up. I was okay with your friends, and I was nervous too."

"Around Ricky and Danny? Come on."

"I was. I'm a well-off white guy with a power job and a suit. They looked at me like I wasn't trustworthy at first, but I won them over, I think. I hope."

Jason nodded. "They like you."

"Listen. This is ideal. You can meet the managing partner and his wife now, one on one; then you won't have anything to worry about when I bring you to the client reception and the holiday party....You'll already be in with the most important people in the room."

"So many parties…" His stomach was in knots. Could he do this?

Teague narrowed his eyes at him. "You're not afraid of a party, are you?"

"Shut up." Jason smiled, though, and shook his head. "You really want your boss to meet me?"

Teague pulled him in suddenly and kissed him hard, setting his heart pounding and making him blush. "I want everyone to meet you."

"I need wine." He got up to find a bottle, Teague's laughter following him out of the room.

"Bring two glasses. Hell, bring the bottle."

"Yes, sir!" Bring the bottle. Right. If it made it that far. He might drink the whole damn thing standing here in the kitchen. Teague wanted him to meet people. Wasn't that Danny's thing? Ask to meet his friends?

He didn't have to ask. He just got invited. He was going to brag so hard.

Take that, Danny.

Not that he was sure he wanted the invitation.

"Are you coming back?" Teague called to him. "Or are you drinking a bottle before you bring me one?"

"Shut up." He so could have. He grabbed the bottle and two glasses and went to his man.

"Couch." Teague took the bottle and opened it, then filled their glasses. "If I can show up with a black eye, you can do this."

He took a long sip of his wine, more like he would from a beer bottle, and swallowed hard, chest burning as he exhaled like he was breathing fire. "Oh. That needed to breathe…"

Teague laughed and sank into the couch next to him. "Of course, with you sitting at the table, they might not even notice my eye. I know I won't want to look at anyone else."

"I'm kind of hoping it will swell up like you're remaking Rocky and no one will even see me." He was only half kidding.

Teague took his hand. "Do you honestly not want to go?"

"No, it's not like that. Of course I want to support you. I've just never been in that kind of company so...under the spotlight." He was nervous. Really nervous.

"Oh, bullshit." Teague shook his head. "It's what you do for a living. Dress up, be fabulous, leave them wanting more."

Huh. Teague did kind of have a point. "What should I wear, though?" He'd text Danny and Ricky. He'd shop if he had to.

"Whatever you wear, I'm bringing you home after and taking you out of it." Teague slid a warm hand over his thigh.

"I like that idea." He leaned in closer. "I like this one too."

20

———

Teague waited anxiously around the corner from the restaurant for Jason. Jason had asked him to so they could walk in together. He wasn't anxious about his black eye, or about bringing Jason—he truly believed that would all be fine—he was anxious because he suddenly understood what people meant when they said, "This is the first day of the rest of your life."

A new position, new responsibility, a new phase of his relationship...he was anxious to get started.

"Hey, Wall Street!" A handsome young man in a sharp blue suit waved to him from across the street and he almost laughed out loud that he didn't immediately recognize Jason.

"Look at you. Oh, my God, Jersey. You...wow. You look—"

"Conservative?"

"Hot. Really fucking hot." *Jesus.* Jason could have worn anything, and he'd have been fine. He would never have asked Jason to dress conservatively, but he sure wasn't complaining. Bucky would be impressed and that suit?

Damn. He pulled his lover in and kissed him. "Eyeliner, huh?"

"Just a little." Jason blinked at him. "Is it too much?"

"No. Nope. You look amazing." Bucky could just deal with eyeliner.

Jason blushed, and his smile lit up the street. "Thank you."

"Are you ready?"

"No, are you?"

"No." He teased, feeling even more confident now. "But I guess two negatives make a positive." He took Jason's arm and tucked it around his. "Come on."

The Midtown steakhouse was busy but as soon as he gave his name, he and Jason were escorted through the dining room to a table near a glassed-in wine room. Bucky and his wife stood, and he smiled, suddenly horrified that he didn't remember her name.

"Teague. Welcome."

"Hi, Bucky. Thank you."

"Teague," Bucky put his arm around a younger woman dressed mostly in black and gray. She was very pretty and had strikingly dark eyes. "This is my wife, Valerie. Darling, this is—hopefully—our newest partner, Teague Whitaker."

He shook hands with Valerie, who had a confident handshake, and shook with Bucky. "Thank you. Bucky, Valerie, this is my partner, Jason."

"Jason. Good to meet you. It's also good to finally know your name." Another round of handshakes and they all sat down.

"Finally?" Jason asked, hands falling gracefully into his lap. Teague was fascinated by Jason's polish.

"Well, I have to admit to being curious after you came to get Teague at the party the other night."

"Oh." Jason chuckled, looking embarrassed. "I'm so sorry about that—"

"Nonsense. Teague's assistant explained about your friend in the hospital. Accidents never happen at convenient times, do they? I hope he's doing better."

Barb?

Flowers. He was going to send her flowers later. A whole shop full. And a Starbucks gift card.

"Kit, yeah." Jason looked even more surprised than he was. "Yes. He's doing a lot better. I called him this morning, and he was in a great mood. Thank you."

Bucky nodded. "Good to hear. So. Teague explained to you why we're all here today, I assume?"

And that was that. How's your friend? Good to meet you. Moving on.

Jesus, he was the luckiest man on earth. Seriously.

"He did. He was very excited. We may have had some wine to celebrate." Jason winked at Bucky.

"Good. That's just what I wanted to hear. And you took care of that bruise? It looks better than I was led to believe."

Shit. He puffed out a breath. "Bucky, I am so embarrassed. Carson just—"

Bucky held up a hand. "Carson is a good lawyer but has professional issues that go deeper than his rivalry with you. I'm sorry you ended up in that position. I trust we can just put all of that behind us?"

He nodded, finding some oxygen at last. "Yes. Yes, thank you. Of course."

"I heard you got in a good swing of your own, though." Valerie smiled at him and gave him a wink.

"I'm never going to live that down now, am I?" Teague dared to grin.

"No. Probably not. Not in small circles, anyway." Bucky

laughed gently. "So you're ready to accept the position I hope?"

"I—yes. Definitely yes. But I do have some questions." He didn't want to seem ungrateful, but he wanted to know... whatever he didn't know.

"Of course you do. We'll talk logistics in my office tomorrow. I'll explain time requirements and how the equity buy-in works and all of that. Today I just wanted to say thank you for a job well done on the Avenstone deal. Kent was very pleased. We'd like you to stick with them as your first personal account."

"Oh, that's—wow. Thank you. I think we have a great working relationship. I understand their business—"

"You do. So, the first thing you need to do after a big closing is plan an outing with the client. Entertain them. Dinner and a show perhaps, or a sporting event and some swag?"

"Kevin loves baseball. He's a big fan."

Bucky nodded his approval. "Then you should reserve our box at Yankee Stadium."

"We have a box at...really?" A box. He was playing in a whole new league now.

So to speak.

"Yes!" Bucky laughed. "More of what we'll talk about tomorrow."

"Great. Thank you." He picked up his water glass.

"Are you a baseball fan, Jason?" Valerie asked, leaning toward Jason. She was kind, trying to keep them both engaged in the conversation.

"No?" Jason shrugged. "I'm not much of a sports fan at all. I'm more the Broadway and cabaret type."

"Valerie loves theater," Bucky offered.

"And we sneak into Neon sometimes. Have you been there?"

Teague shook his head. "No, I've never heard—"

Jason smiled. "Yes. Of course I have. It's *amazing*."

"You'd fit right in with your eyeliner."

Jason leaned toward her this time. "I didn't go too heavy, did I? I just wanted my eyes to pop a little. This suit is so...blue."

Valerie studied Jason's face. "No. No, I don't think so. I think it's handsome. My godson wears it very heavily. He plays guitar."

"If you can call what he does playing. I can't find the music in all the noise." Bucky rolled his eyes, and they all laughed.

This was going much better than he'd dreamed it could.

Bucky had ordered for the table before they'd arrived and three beautiful steaks, plus a lovely salmon dish were set in front of them. His mouth was literally watering, and he hadn't even picked up his fork yet.

"Valerie doesn't eat beef. Are you all right, Jason? Would you prefer something else?"

Jason's eyes were huge. "This looks delicious to me. I'm going to have to take a doggie bag, though, I'll never finish it."

Bucky dug into his right away. "Slice it up for sandwiches tomorrow. It makes excellent leftovers."

"Tell me, Teague, how did the two of you meet?"

Teague smiled at Valerie and finished chewing, noting that Jason wasn't trying to field that question for him. He wasn't worried. "We met at the bar where Jason works the night I thought I'd lost the Avenstone deal."

"I could tell he'd had a bad day." Jason nodded and patted his thigh.

"It wasn't a good one, to be sure."

Bucky shook his head. "You should have called me, Teague. If you had, I would have told you that I knew you'd done everything you could in the client's interest. We all had our eyes on you; I'd followed everything you were doing."

"You did?" God, he'd have been a wreck if he'd known that.

Which was probably why he hadn't known.

"Of course. As your mentor, that's my job. Look. Sometimes, it doesn't matter how much work you put in. Deals fall through. It happens to all of us."

He looked at Bucky. "I thought I'd disappointed the client. I thought...well, I thought you'd probably fire me."

Bucky nodded, but it was underscored by a knowing laugh. "It was your first big deal, Teague. You're young. I understand that you felt that way, but nothing could have been further from reality. Trust that as partner, no one is going to call for your resignation over a deal that falls apart. Next time, you make sure to talk to me before you panic."

"I will." He took a deep breath, feeling both relieved and a little embarrassed. "I definitely will."

"Though if you hadn't panicked and gone to that bar...?" Valerie teased and picked up her wine and took a sip.

"Silver linings," he replied and took Jason's hand. "I was obviously where I was meant to be."

Jason's blush made him smile. He knew this was awkward for his lover, but Jason was handling it so well. Teague was as impressed as he was grateful. And a little turned-on, too.

Dessert arrived, and they all groaned. All but Bucky, who picked up his glass and caught Teague's eye. "Here's to a new chapter with the firm, Whitaker. Congratulations."

Everyone picked up their glasses.

"Let's see if you can get through your first year without another shiner." Bucky's eyes twinkled, and they all laughed.

He felt like he could relax now. Hell, this was a celebration, right?

Maybe he could find room for a bite of cheesecake.

21

J ason leaned on Teague and they climbed up out of the
subway. It was finally fall, and the heat that had hung
over the city all summer was gone, so he turned his
face into the sun as they hit the sidewalk. "Oh. Nice day."

"Great day." Teague took his hand.

"Yeah. That went pretty well, huh?"

"It was perfect. You were amazing. They loved you."

"Valerie sure liked me." He shook his head, grinning. "I
could totally see me shopping with her. Or...for her. I
probably can't afford the places she shops."

"Someday. When your temporary, live-in boyfriend—"

"Ah! Stop right there." Jason smiled, teasing. "You are not
temporary, and I am the live-in."

Teague laughed. "I stand corrected. After you have
moved in with the handsome new partner at a pricey New
York law firm—temporarily on a permanent basis—and he
gets his first bonus—"

"On a permanent basis?" Jason sighed. "Teague. Don't
make fun of me. I need this."

"I know, Jersey cowboy. I know." Teague tugged him

closer. "You can call it temporary for as long as you need to, but I know better."

How could he possibly know better? "What if doesn't work?"

"It will." Such confidence.

"What if I change my mind? Hm?" Jason raised an eyebrow.

"You won't."

Teague was so self-assured. It was almost as scary as it was comforting. "Well...what if *you* do?"

Teague stopped them in the middle of the sidewalk. He could imagine how annoyed people around them were, but he didn't worry about it. The last time they did this, the kiss led to something amazing. Teague had his full attention.

"I won't change my mind."

He searched Teague's face for answers. "How do you know?"

"Because it's not my mind that's so sure about you. It's my heart."

"Teague." His whole world, his whole being, every nerve in his body focused on this amazing man. The first man to truly see him, to understand him. The first one to want all of him. He was about to say more, but Teague distracted him with a kiss so sweet that whatever it was went right out of his head.

Or, okay. Into his other one. Like *whoa*.

"You need to take me home right now."

"I was trying to, but you kept *talking* and *talking*." Teague shook his head.

He licked his lips and tried to swallow, but his mouth had gone dry. "I won't say another fucking word."

Someone bumped into his shoulder and he tumbled into Teague, making them both laugh.

Teague hooked an arm around him, and they started walking again. "I'm not trying to pressure you, I promise."

"You're trying to turn me on, though." And that was okay by him.

"Maybe. I did promise to undress you when we got home."

"You did." He blushed and dropped his head on Teague's shoulder as they walked.

"Slowly."

Jesus. The growl in Teague's voice made him shiver. "I might like that part."

"Oh, yes. Piece by piece," Teague purred at him. "I might even make you wait while I fold them."

"Dork." But Teague could say anything in that voice, and it would turn him on.

"I just want to celebrate."

Jason lifted his head and pulled Teague along. "You should. You got a promotion! We can go out tonight."

"And us. I want to celebrate *us*."

"We can do that." He turned on a little heat of his own, giving Teague bedroom eyes. "I want to celebrate all over you."

His lover swallowed and almost stumbled. "Oh, look. We're home." Teague dragged him through the doors. Jason let himself enjoy the moment and grinned smugly, knowing he'd hit a nerve.

"Would you look at that? Hello!" He waved at the security guard in the lobby. "Oh look, it's not Chrissy."

"Did you say something?" Teague kept very close and hustled him into the elevator.

Had he? "Maybe. Who cares?" He tangled his fingers in Teague's tie and kissed him. He swore he could taste the need on his lover's tongue.

They parted reluctantly as the doors opened again, staring at each other as they both took a dazed breath, then made their way to Teague's apartment—his apartment? *Their* apartment. He chuckled as Teague fumbled with the key, fingers trembling, as turned-on as he was.

"Open the door, baby, I need you," he whispered, knowing full well it would make things worse, not better.

"Fuck. Fuck! Stupid key." Teague took another breath. "Okay. I've got this." The key slid into the lock and the door opened wide, knocking into the entry hall table and making the lamp wobble.

"Got it!" Jason dashed in and caught the lamp just as it toppled over and set it upright. The door slammed closed behind him and Teague pounced on him, the momentum knocking him back. The lamp went over sideways this time, and he was dimly aware of it falling again, but Teague's heavy cock was hard and wanting against his ass, and he just didn't give a damn.

"Yes. Yes, please," he begged. Teague's fingers loosened his belt, and the fancy new trousers he was wearing fell around his ankles. He barely had time to register it, though—Teague's hand slipped into his briefs and caught his cock up tight. "Fuck!"

"So hot in this suit, turned me on as soon as I saw you. All I could think about at lunch was getting you out of it." Teague stroked him and rocked into him again.

He braced one hand on the wall above the little table, ignoring how it tipped up on two legs every time Teague moved. Pens, mail, keys fell to the floor. "Oh. Oh, God. Please, Teague."

Teague pulled his hand away and tore the suit jacket off Jason's shoulders. Jason toed his dress shoes off and kicked the trousers away, then arched, shoving at Teague with his ass so he could turn around. They worked on their ties, fingers flying and eyes locked, heat and intensity building between them.

Teague threw his tie and started in on the buttons of his dress shirt. "Any hotter, we'd burn this place to the ground."

"Let's find out." He dropped his tie and pushed Teague into the opposite wall. The small foyer wasn't going to hold them for long. He finished with Teague's shirt and pushed it open, lips finding a nipple and sucking it in hard.

"Fuck! Jason..."

"Mhm." He moved to the other one, showing no mercy. He knew what his lover liked.

"Fuck. Get me a rubber," Teague demanded breathlessly.

"Not your errand boy," he teased, pressing a hand into Teague's groin.

Teague groaned. "You're going to suck me with that smart mouth."

"Oh, yeah?" He stepped away with a saucy sway, backing down the hall toward the bedroom. He was hard as nails and Teague was stalking him, staring at him hungrily, but he flirted and played, loving Teague all hot and bothered, impatient. He took his own shirt off outside the bedroom door. "Make me."

Teague dumped his shirt and growled, chasing him down and catching him by the nape. Teague's kiss was hard and hungry, taking what he needed and turning Jason's knees to jelly. He moaned and swayed, but Teague caught him with a strong arm. He slipped to his knees, so ready for a taste, and impatiently helped Teague get free of his trousers. The second he could, he tugged Teague's briefs off and tasted the length of his ruddy cock.

Fuck, Teague was granite hard and nearly howled at the

hot touch of his tongue. He took it easy, just teasing because they both wanted so much more.

"Yes. Oh God, yes." Teague praised him, fingers curling under his chin and helping him hold back. "Just...so good."

He lost himself in the gentle attention, loving Teague's sounds, making his lover feel good. He could keep this up forever.

But Teague had other ideas.

He was suddenly on his feet and he blinked, disoriented. Teague spun him and his arms shot out instinctively, bracing against the wall to keep from falling. He heard the foil tear, and only felt a few seconds of cool lube before Teague's fingers breached him, slicking him quickly and purposefully. "Yes! More. Want you. Please, baby."

"Jason." The fingers disappeared, replaced instantly by Teague. The hard cock pushed in steadily, and they both groaned heavily as Jason adjusted to his lover's coveted intrusion. "Fuck, so good. Want you."

"Got me." Teague rocked into him balls deep, then pulled out and dove in again, hips finally settling into a heavy rhythm.

The burn was everything he wanted. He arched and welcomed Teague over and over until his moans were deep and constant and Teague was trembling, thrusts coming shallow and fast. Jason curled his fingers around his aching prick and one good squeeze was all it took. "Baby, coming. Fuck!"

Teague gripped him tighter with a strangled shout, hips working hard and fast. A few more thrusts pushed him over, and they were gasping and panting together, both braced against the wall so they didn't topple like the hall table lamp.

After a still moment, Teague's prick twitched and jerked

inside him and they both moaned as his lover slipped free. Teague pulled him in and took him to bed, whispering soft words in his ear. Teague cleaned up and joined him, climbing in at his back and curling around him, holding him tight.

"Love you," Teague said in a soft and sated voice.

His response was easy because it was truthful. "I love you, baby."

He knew. Teague was right. There was nothing temporary between them. Nothing at all. He belonged to this beautiful, kind, loving man, no matter how strange and difficult to believe. They weren't really worlds apart. The universe just hadn't figured out their secret yet.

EPILOGUE

J esus, what a day.

Teague loosened his tie and slid his butt onto a stool at the bar. He pulled out his wallet and set a credit card down, sliding it over to the bartender with a smile. Elliot was on tonight, and he and Teague had become friendly over the last couple of months. "Whiskey sour."

"Dallas says your drinks are on him."

Teague grinned at Elliot. "I know, but take the card anyway."

"Nope. Not tonight, birthday boy." Elliot slid it back to him with a wink.

Uh-oh. "Does everybody know?"

"Yep. Everyone." Elliot laughed as he poured Teague's drink. "Should be fun."

Oh, boy. What had he walked into? No wonder Jason insisted they meet up at the club after work.

"Wall Street!" He turned on his stool to greet Danny, who moved toward him gracefully, surrounded by a riot of feathers. Danny leaned in and kissed his cheek. "Happy Birthday."

"Thank you." He returned the cheek-kiss. Danny was nothing like anyone he'd ever known, but he was a good man and a loyal friend to Jason. Teague liked him very much.

"Jason says you're officially thirty-five."

He sighed. "Old, I know."

"Wise, honey. They're solid years. You earned them."

Teague appreciated the compliment. He'd worked hard to make sure Jason's friends trusted him. "Tell me that when you're thirty-five."

"Let's see how thirty goes first. A few years from now." Danny did a cheeky little dance.

"Ugh." He rolled his eyes. "Babies. I'm surrounded by babies."

"Ricky is thirty."

"Oh, I feel *much* better." He didn't at all. But he did feel like he'd earned his years, and he had a lot to show for them.

"Gentlemen, and not-so-gentle-men!"

The crowd groaned.

"We have a very special treat for you. Tonight, we have a VIP in the house."

Danny patted his knee. "Good luck, honey."

"Good luck?" He'd been waiting for the other shoe to drop since Elliot had warned him, and drop it did—in classic Jersey cowboy fashion.

The spotlights did a ballyhoo as loud bluegrass music filled the club. It was strange and incongruous until the DJ filled it in with a thumping beat, a mashup that worked better than it probably should have. The spotlights finally stopped at the far end of the bar and he blinked at the empty spot where Jason, as Dallas, usually appeared, surprised not to see him there. The lights shifted suddenly and there was Jason, sitting on the barstool next to his. Another spotlight landed on *him*. The bright light made his eyes water, and all he could see was his man—his Jersey cowboy—looking as sexy as ever in cutoffs and boots.

"Happy Birthday, Wall Street!" Jason shouted. Someone stuck a hat on his head, and he reached for it to get a look. It was a pink and glittery cowboy hat with a band that said "Birthday Boy" on it.

He chuckled and, trying to be a good sport, stuck it back on his head. "Yeehaw!"

Jason laughed and climbed into his lap. "That's my line!" A second later a country singer broke into "Happy Birthday."

"Dwight Yoakam," Jason said in his ear. He'd known nothing about country music two months ago, but as soon as Jason moved in with him, he'd learned quickly. His lover was a real fan.

As soon as Jason started singing along, so did the rest of the club.

The whole club. Singing. To him.

A couple of burly guys lifted Jason onto the bar, then came for him. "No." He waved his hand. "No, no. Wait, guys, I'm good. Really. Oh, my God." His protests were useless as he was lifted like he weighed nothing whether he wanted to be up there or not.

"Hey, Wall Street." Jason's smile was bright, blinding him more than the spotlights.

"Hey, Jersey cowboy." He was so in love he had no hope of hiding it, and he didn't want to.

Jason moved in close. "I'm going to kiss you."

Oh, what the hell. "No, I'm going to kiss you." He took Jason's face in both hands and kissed his Jersey cowboy shamelessly, giving Jason a surprise of his own.

The crowd applauded for them, but the sound was muted and barely registered. All of his focus was on his lover, his Jersey cowboy, his Dallas, his Jason, his love. His proudest accomplishment.

His partner.

The most important deal he'd ever land.

When they finally parted, Jason laughed and started to dance. He relaxed and did his best to keep up. Once again. He might never manage it, but he planned to die happy trying.

When the song ended and the lights shifted to Danny on stage, they were each helped down from the bar. Jason's fingers went for his tie, loosened it, and pulled it out of his collar. "You don't need this. It's time to relax, Wall Street. It's your birthday."

"Relax, huh? After that display?" He caught Jason's fingers and kissed them.

Jason gave him a playful pout. "I had to celebrate you. You don't turn thirty-five every day. You were a good sport."

"Thank you. It was fun. Really. You're always surprising me."

"That's the plan." Jason kissed him quickly. "But first, I have to work, baby."

"I know. I'll be right here." He let Jason go reluctantly.

"Watching?"

"Admiring."

Teague didn't need reassuring; Jason's blush told him everything he needed to know. "Later, Wall Street."

"I work in Midtown!" Not that it mattered. His place was wherever Jason wanted him to be.

THE END

Keeping Promises
By Jodi Payne and BA Tortuga

Jeremy M. Dunn III has the single dad thing down, so the last thing he wants to do is call his ex-husband to ask for help with their two kids. They didn't part on good terms, and they've barely spoken since the divorce. But with a cast on his arm that goes up past his elbow, Jeremy has no choice. He needs a few days to figure out how to bathe their daughter, make school lunches and parent their son one-armed, and there isn't anyone else he can ask for help.

Former rodeo cowboy West Belen was already on his way back to his kids, and to Trey ("the third", his nickname for Jeremy). He made a promise to try again, and he means to keep it, so when he sees his chance to move back into his family's life, he grabs it like the brass ring he knows it is. He's determined to be more than an "every other weekend" dad to his children, and he doesn't want to keep on living with regret about how he and Trey ended.

Jeremy still desires West, but he isn't sure he can trust West to be responsible and available. West still thinks Trey is the hottest thing he's ever seen, but he has no idea how to convince the man he's ready to settle down. The two of them have never had trouble butting heads, but now they need to learn to work together to make a home for themselves and their kids where they both belong.

NEW, Released March 23 , 2021!

A NOTE FROM THE AUTHOR

Hey there!

I just wanted to take a minute to say thank you for taking the time to read Mergers & Acquisitions. I hope you enjoyed it. I know everyone is busy and our TBR (to be read) lists are out of control, so it means a lot to me that I ended up at the top of your pile this time.

If you have a moment, please consider dropping by the site where you purchased this book and leaving a review. All honest reviews are much appreciated.

If you're looking for more of my work, why not join my newsletter? Just go here: http://bit.ly/whatsupjodi.

ABOUT JODI

JODI takes herself way too seriously and has been known to randomly break out in song. Her men are imperfect but genuine, stubborn but likable, often kinky, and frequently their own worst enemies. They are characters you can't help but fall in love with while they stumble along the path to their happily ever after. For those looking to get on her good side, Jodi's addictions include nonfat lattes, Malbec and tequila any way you pour it.

Website: jodipayne.net
Newsletter: http://bit.ly/whatsupjodi
All Jodi's Social Links: linktr.ee/jodipayne

Interested in learning more about Jodi's gentlemen? Want free fiction and news? Join my newsletter!

What's Up with Jodi
http://bit.ly/whatsupjodi

MORE BOOKS BY JODI

M/M Romance
Stable Hill
Soft Limits: A Deviations Novel
Creative Process
Linchpin
Whence He Came
Mergers & Acquisitions

With BA Tortuga
Les's Bar Series
Just Dex

The Triskelion Series
Breaking the Rules

East Meets Westerns
(single titles)
Heart of a Redneck
Wrecked
Land of Enchantment
Window Dressing
Flying Blind
Special Delivery, A Wrecked Holiday Novel
Keeping Promises

The Cowboy and the Dom Trilogy
First Rodeo, Book One
Razor's Edge, Book Two

No Ghosts, Book Three
The Soldier and the Angel, a Cowboy and Dom Novel

The Collaborations Series
Refraction
Syncopation

With Chris Owen
The Deviations Series
Submission
Domination
Discipline
Bondage
Safe Words

F/F Romance
Best Lesbian Love Stories, Summer Flings
Sapphic Planet